DENIAL

DENIAL

LORNA SCHULTZ NICHOLSON

JAMES LORIMER & COMPANY LTD., PUBLISHERS
TORONTO

James Lorimer & Company Ltd., Publishers acknowledges funding support from
the Ontario Arts Council (OAC), an agency of the Government of Ontario. We
acknowledge the support of the Canada Council for the Arts, which last year
invested $153 million to bring the arts to Canadians throughout the country. This
project has been made possible in part by the Government of Canada and with the
support of Ontario Creates.

Cover design: Tyler Cleroux
Cover image: Shutterstock

Library and Archives Canada Cataloguing in Publication (Paperback)

Title: Denial / Lorna Schultz Nicholson.
Names: Schultz Nicholson, Lorna, author.
Identifiers: Canadiana (print) 2021026764X | Canadiana (ebook) 20210267666 |
ISBN 9781459416710 (softcover) | ISBN 9781459416727 (EPUB)
Classification: LCC PS8637.C58 D46 2022 | DDC C813/.6—dc23

Published by:
James Lorimer &
Company Ltd.,
Publishers
117 Peter Street, Suite 304
Toronto, ON, Canada
M5V 0M3
www.lorimer.ca

Distributed in Canada by:
Formac Lorimer Books
5502 Atlantic Street
Halifax, NS, Canada
B3H 1G4
www.formac.ca

Distributed in the US by:
Lerner Publisher Services
241 1st Ave. N.
Minneapolis, MN, USA
55401
www.lernerbooks.com

Printed and bound in Canada.
Manufactured by Friesens in Altona, MB in December 2021.
Job # 284839

PART ONE

MAY 9

Blood pools on the floor and little droplets trickle down a beige wall. I stare down at my grey hoodie and see the traces there as well, crimson streaks that look like red ribbons. Only they're not pretty ribbons that are meant for pretty hair. No. This is blood. Blood. How can there be so much blood? And my sweatpants are even worse. Everything is starting to feel sticky and gross, and it makes me want to throw up. A raw smell stings my nostrils.

I walk back and forth, muttering to myself. What have I done? What have I done? What have I done? Back and forth. My movements slow, not fast. My limbs feel like they are filled with heavy sand. My feet plod over the floor. One foot, then the other. Over and over. Back and forth.

I stop. I have to. I make myself assess the situation. Now I speak out loud, my voice echoes as I'm alone. No one will answer me. "Ohmygod! Ohmygod!" My voice escalates, and I can hear it screaming. "What am I going to do?!"

Big breath in. Big breath out. First things first. I need to clean up and destroy evidence. I walk to the linen closet, hardly aware that I'm moving. I get a towel, get down on my hands and knees and start swishing it back and forth, watching as the colour of it changes from white to pink. My movements pick up speed, my arms now pumping.

Then the thought hits me . . . what will I do with the towel? I sit back on my heels. The laundry room in this stupid apartment I live in is downstairs. I can't do the laundry down there, wash this towel or my clothes. What if someone comes in and asks why the towel has so much blood on it?

Throw it out.

I stand and go get a green garbage bag from the kitchen drawer. I stuff the towel into the bag. Since my clothes are bloody too, I strip down to my underwear, throwing my sweatsuit in the green bag. A cold breeze circles me and I start to shiver uncontrollably. I wrap my arms around my chest, hoping to make my body stop shaking. My eyes burn with tears that need to be shed.

My knees buckle, and I crumple to the floor. Sobs escape from my body. Sobs I can't stop. My shoulders shake and the tears are like a faucet.

But then . . . the nagging question returns. What have I done?

I wipe the tears with the back of my hand. "Get it together, Nova."

I have to fix this somehow.

I push myself to stand. Even in my dazed state, I know what needs to be done. I just don't know if I can do it. First, I need to put on some clean clothes. I go to my room and grab a pair of black sweats from the dirty laundry hamper, and an old T-shirt.

Where is my phone?

I remember dropping it by the front door. Like a zombie, I walk to the front door, see my phone and pick it up. Even it is covered in blood. I should wash my hands. No. First, I must do what I need to do. Then I will clean my phone.

I press nine. Stop. Then I press a one. Stop. I stare at my phone. No. I can't call the police just yet. I just can't. Think, Nova, think. You have to do something.

I only have one option. Before I can chicken out completely, and ruin my life for good, I need to call someone. Who? Who should I call?

The voice on the other end is groggy — after all it is Thailand time. "Nova?"

"Brad," I say, my voice quivering, my body shaking. "I need your help." My words rush out of my mouth. "I'm in trouble. I've done something awful."

CHAPTER 1
LAST SEPTEMBER

Music blares. Voices laugh, some low, some shrill. The noise is at an ear-splitting decibel. Red cups litter the countertops. And, like at any high school party, couples grope in corners. I'm one of the ones in the corner, only I'm with my boyfriend and not some hookup. I won't have to do the walk of shame at school on Monday morning.

I lean against the wall. Leo touches my hair, running his fingers through the long, brown strands. Our bodies are pressed together. We are close. Real close. I bet you couldn't put a piece of paper between us. I look up at him, and he leans down and kisses me. So gently. His lips taste sweet, maybe like rum and Coke. I kiss him back, and my body reacts. I tremble, in a really good way.

"Why don't you two just get a room already," my best friend, Izzy, shouts from across the room.

I pull back from Leo and look up at him. We burst out laughing. I touch my swollen lips. Then I turn to see Izzy grinning. Her dark bob haircut bounces with the shake of her head.

"We could go upstairs," whispers Leo in my ear.

"Upstairs?" I whisper back.

After sticking my tongue out at Izzy, I once again stare into Leo's brown eyes. My heart pounds under my cotton blouse. In a good way and a bad way. Yes, I do want to go upstairs, be alone. I'm ready. Oh yeah, I'm more than ready. Leo is my guy, the one I've been waiting for. We're in love. Everyone knows we're the power couple in our high school. Leo and Nova are two words that go together like steamed milk in a latte.

Leo takes my hand, intertwining our fingers. Every time he touches me, it's like a fire burns inside me, warming my entire being. I like the heat. Oh, yes, I do. With my hand in his, he starts walking through the kitchen, past Izzy. I look at her and she mouths, "What's going on?"

I shrug, giggle and continue to follow Leo, my toes almost touching his heels.

The path to the stairs is full of people. Bodies crammed everywhere. The party is at the house of a school friend who is also on the swim team. His parents are out of town. Leo doesn't let go of my hand, but our tight grasp slips. Now only his baby finger is linked with mine. Even with such a simple touch, I can still feel the electricity passing through us. I keep following him and we move through the living room, which has turned into a makeshift dance floor. Sweaty bodies gyrate and pulse to the downbeat. Leo turns and flashes his smile, lighting my heart, making it pulse.

We hit the stairs. I don't look around to see if anyone is watching us. I just stare at Leo's muscular butt. He's the best swimmer in our school, the entire city, and is a to-watch-for National Team prospect. Next year, after we graduate, he's off to the University of Michigan to swim on a scholarship. I'm on the high school swim team too, but have no desire to continue swimming. I want to get a science degree and get into medical school, maybe even be a surgeon, like my heroes on *Grey's Anatomy*. I can imagine us later in life, both successful, still together.

My gaze travels from his long legs, upward, to his V-shaped

back. Such broad shoulders from his years of the butterfly stroke. Since I'm five foot ten, it's so nice to have a guy who is taller than me. My height has always been the reason for zero dates. Until six-foot-three Leo came along.

Of all the girls he could have picked, he picked me.

"What if someone is in the bedroom?" I whisper, giggling.

"Don't worry," he says. "Carl told everyone his room is off-limits. We're good to go."

"Make sure it's Carl's room," I say. "Not his parents' room. That would be nasty."

Leo flashes his white teeth in a sexy smile. "Don't worry. I got this."

He opens the door to a room at the end of the hall, pulling me in. The door shuts behind us. The room is dark, but I can see outlines of stuff like trophies, medals, posters. I giggle, but it's a funny, almost nervous giggle. Like a twitter or something. Everything about this seems so bad. Naughty. Wrong.

He kisses me.

I kiss him back. I want *it* to happen. I've been waiting. But since I've waited so long, I'm just not sure we're in the right place. I want it to be perfect.

He presses against me. We grind a little bit. We've done this before, but not much else. Well, maybe a few other little things, but not *it*. I know Leo wants more. We've been dating for five months now. He leads me over to the bed, and in the dark I see a Raptors basketball duvet cover. Do I really want to make love for my first time on Carl's bed? On some sports duvet? A little sliver of moonlight shines through the window.

As I lie down on my back, it feels weird to be on this strange bed. Leo lies down beside me and we kiss some more. Like a lot more. Our mouths are like magnets stuck together. His hands roam all over my body, then he undoes a button on my blouse.

Another button. And another. Oh god, this is really going to happen. But something doesn't feel right. I'm in some random room on some guy's Raptors duvet. Kinda gross. Then it hits me. What if someone already did this before us? What if Carl is giving out his bedroom to all the best guys on the swim team?

Suddenly, my top is off completely. Cold air sweeps over me, and I want to cover myself.

"It's okay," Leo whispers. "You're so beautiful."

A big ball of something gets wedged in my throat. I nod because I can't speak. He whips his shirt off. We press together, our skin touching. We roll around for a few seconds.

Then he goes for the zipper on my jeans. Suddenly, I freeze. All that warm air heating my insides is now cold. I swear I can feel a balled-up sock under my back. Or even worse . . . what if it's underwear? *Ewwww.*

"No." The word just blurts out of my mouth. "Not here."

He pulls away from me, and exhales.

"Nova, you're killing me. You know that, right?" Our foreheads touch.

Again, the ball is in my throat, but I manage to squeak out, "Soon." I take a breath, dislodge the ball and say, "Not in this room. I want our first time to be perfect." I grab my bra and blouse and start to get dressed. "Anyway, I'm not on the pill, yet."

He sits up, runs his hand through his hair and groans. "Okay," he says. "But I was going to use a condom."

My hands shaking, I continue doing up my blouse buttons.

He exhales, and exhales again, obviously trying to get his hormones in check. After a few seconds, he looks around the room. Then he suddenly just starts laughing. Like howling.

"What's so funny?"

He points across the room. "Carl's still got bobble-heads. Look on that shelf." He shakes his head. "He's been collecting those NBA heads since grade school."

I look over at the trophy shelf on the wall. I see basketball bobble-heads lined up like fans. I swear they're moving. For some reason this seems hilarious to me too. "The bobble-heads are staring at us." I start to howl. "Ohmygod. They're so creepy. It's like they're watching us."

Both of us are now in hysterics. We flop back on the bed. He tickles me. I squirm and grab my stomach, I'm laughing so hard.

"We almost did it," I say, breathless, "with a bobble-head audience. They're like voyeurs."

"I'm going to get him good for this," says Leo. He pops up. "Back to the party?"

I nod, my head bobbing like one of the stupid bobble-heads. *God, what were we thinking?* I want magic, not some creepy room with bobble heads.

"I've still got vodka stashed," I say.

He grabs my hand and pulls me to standing. "Let's head," he says. As we walk out, he grabs a bobble-head off the shelf.

CHAPTER 2
ALWAYS THE SAME TALK

"So . . . I'm going on the pill," I say to Izzy.

We're in my bedroom with country music playing, and she's knitting, the needles clicking. I'm lying on my back, my head a bit fuzzy from the party the night before. I snuck in at midnight, which is hard to do in the small apartment I now live in.

"How close did you get?" Izzy asks without looking up. Her concentration is on the purple yarn she's making into socks.

"Close."

"How close?"

"Close."

"Like clothes-off close?"

I throw a pillow at her. "Stop!"

She ducks but her needles keep clicking. "Yeah, get on the pill."

"You think it'll make me fat?"

Izzy stops knitting, looks at me and laughs. "Nooooo. Who told you that? I've been on it for a year now and didn't put on an ounce."

"Yeah, but that's you. You're the size of a short pencil." I pause. "I heard Ainsley talking about it in the change room."

"Oh, for god's sakes." Izzy shakes her head. "She's always worried about being fat. Whatever."

"Yeah, true enough."

"Just go to a clinic. It's super easy." She wraps up her knitting, rolling purple yarn around more purple yarn. "They ask a few questions and then give you a prescription. It'll help get your wacky periods in line too, ya know. Or at least it should."

"Good to know." Since I started swimming with the high school swim team three years ago, my periods have been weird. The doctor suggested the pill, but my mother refused, saying, "My daughter will not be put on the pill at such a young age." She's got some old-fashioned views on sex that stem from her staunch Catholic upbringing, and a bad experience with a "boy" who is my half-brother's deadbeat dad.

I watch Izzy stuff her knitting into her special knitting bag. Izzy had sex with her first boyfriend when she was fifteen. It was a boyfriend she'd dated for a year, but still. Here's me, seventeen, and still a virgin. But I wanted to wait until I found the right guy, and Leo is the one.

Me and Izzy are different that way. Well, we're different in a lot of ways. I'm five foot ten, she's five foot two. I'm white, she's Korean. She's built like a rake, and I've got a swimmer's build. I like sports, and she likes to knit. Despite all our differences, we've been best friends since elementary school. Her parents came over from Korea and Izzy was born in Canada. We met on our first day of kindergarten and became fast friends. Even then I was way taller than her, but we just clicked. We're like that saying, "Opposites attract."

"I'm happy for you and Leo," she says.

"Yeah, me too." I jokingly put my hands together like I'm praying. "Please. Soon."

Izzy stands. Then she pretends to swoon, dropping to my bed so the springs bounce.

I laugh. "Oh, stop."

"Okay, okay," she says laughing with me. "I gotta go. I got a crapload of homework to do." She gets off my bed.

"Me too," I say. "Physics is brutal right now. I've still got a lab to write up."

"Don't the teachers know we're in senior year?" Izzy moans. "God, they've been giving so much homework and we're like only three weeks into the year."

"Getting us ready for university," I say.

"You're a genius, though. Lucky you. I got fifty-four per cent on my last math quiz and my mother found it and freaked out. One test and she is convinced I'm doomed for failure." She holds her hand to her throat. "Now I'm on a leash."

Izzy leaves, but I don't do my homework. Instead, I lie on my bed and stare at the peeling paint on the ceiling, thinking about what I'm about to do. Izzy is right. I need to go on the pill. Leo and I are in love, so it's time.

How am I going to keep this from Mom, though? I can't tell her. Not since she's been yapping at me to "be careful" and "save sex for later." It's so annoying when she starts up. She got preggers in grade eleven and didn't even graduate high school. It didn't help that my grandparents weren't exactly supportive and, being over-the-top religious, abortion was definitely out of the equation. They made her get married to some loser who drank all the time. She got out of that one after he hit her, but was a single mom until she met my dad. Now all she cares about are *my* marks, *my* future and *me* keeping some perfect, clean image.

I'll just have to hide the pills in some discreet location. I glance around my small room. None of my furniture fit when we had to move to this dingy apartment building. My double bed and dresser that worked so nicely in my last room, in our *house,* look like they're squeezed into the tightest jeans ever, and fat is spilling over the sides. And my homework desk got sold for a hundred dollars (I didn't get to even keep the money from the sale), and we went to IKEA and bought the smallest desk possible. And the cheapest.

I sigh. Whatever. It is what it is.

My thoughts go back to the now and going to a clinic, walking in a door and asking a stranger to prescribe me birth control pills. My heart does this weird racing. I sit up and lean against my headboard. Maybe I could go right now and get this over with. It's a bus ride, but it is only three in the afternoon. I could get there in thirty minutes and still be home by dinner. I log on to my laptop to check out the hours. Closed Sundays. Okay, so I will have to go tomorrow after school. I put my laptop on the floor, and my eyelids droop, my body sinking into my sheets.

Next thing I know, my mother is calling me for dinner. I wipe the saliva off my mouth and get out of bed. Then I see the time. Crap. It's six and I didn't make a dent in my homework. Food first. I groan because I know it's going to be a long night.

Something smells great when I walk into the kitchen, even though we're having the leftover lasagna that I made a few days ago. With Mom picking up extra shifts as a caregiver in a nursing home, and Dad gone all the time, I've been chipping in with the cooking. Mom has added garlic toast, and that's the smell I'm excited about. Good hangover food.

"How was work?" I ask.

"Long." She almost sighs. How someone can *almost sigh* is beyond me, but my mother can.

I don't reply. Lately, things have been a bit rough around our place. Her life hasn't been easy with my dad losing his job over a year ago now, so I try to stay neutral. He was a senior manager at a communications company, and they let him go to cut costs. Mom picks up shifts to make ends meet.

I open the cupboard where the plates are stored. She always says my dad saved her from her single-mother life, but now I'm not so sure she's feeling all the love. I'm guessing this move from house to apartment has put her in a bad place again. The mortgage payments were a struggle with Dad not pulling in the big paycheque, so we sold our house in twenty-four hours and now we rent this small three-bedroom apartment on Davisville. I've been told it's a short-term arrangement before they make their decision on the next step. The only good thing about the apartment is we're close to the Yonge Street subway line. The kitchen is small, the walls are thin and the halls stink. All. The. Time.

"Dad home?" I ask.

"No. He picked up an extra shift."

I take out two plates. My dad has spent a year looking for jobs, going to interviews and coming close. Since he's not one to sit around and mope, he recently got a job at the local hardware store. Between his strange hours, and my mom working extra hours, the three of us are never in the same room at the same time.

I set the table and we sit down to eat. Silence circles us like a floating bubble. If I popped the thing it would splat on top of us. Blue bags hang under my mom's eyes. I don't want to add more stress to her life, so I'll never tell her I'm going on the pill. She'll freak, even though it's the right move. I mean, she got drunk in high school and ended up pregnant. If she would have gone on the pill, she could have dodged that one and gone on and got a real career.

"You were late last night," she says.

"Yeah."

"Were you drinking?"

I shrug. I want to lie and say no but instead I say, "A little."

She does this weird nod and purses her lips. I wait. I know it's coming.

"Don't get into that habit," she says. "I can tell you it'll ruin your future."

"Mom, please. Let's not do this again. I'm in senior year. Cut me some slack."

She looks at me, making eye contact. "You're underage. Focus on school. You need a career."

"Um, so far, my grades are great. I haven't got below a ninety on anything. I'm striving to win the academic award."

"It's only September. Those parties can catch up to you."

"Oh my god, Mom. We're two different people. And things have changed since you were in high school." I pause. "You could go back to school, you know." I tell her this all the time.

"Don't change the subject," she says. "Some things are the same in every era." This time she really sighs.

I wish she would go back, do something for herself. Suddenly, the garlic toast I wanted so badly doesn't taste that good. I pick at my lasagna, spreading it around my plate.

"I'm sorry," she says. "I do sound like I'm on repeat. It's just that you have so much potential."

I shove a forkful of lasagna in my mouth, staring at my plate. Again, I wait. Another conversation is coming. Lately, if we're not talking about me ruining my life by partying in senior year, we're talking about the other thing. If I eat, I can get out of here quicker, and to my room to shut the door.

"It's just that —"

"— stop." I hold up my hands, palms out to her. "Let's not talk about Brad, either."

My older half-brother Brad (the out-of-wedlock baby) is trying to find himself on a beach in Thailand after dropping out of university. The part that made my parents freak was how he wasted their hard-earned money. They set it aside for his university tuition, and even gave him spending money. Which he used for a plane ticket that they knew nothing about. He texted when he was already in Thailand. I guess smoking pot and whatever else he can score is his new university course. They put a lot of pressure on him, and he caved. What he did was wrong in my eyes, mainly because he got money to go away to school, and they've spent mine to make ends meet. I'm stuck in Toronto next year for university. But he's still my brother and I miss him.

"I wish he'd call more," she says.

I don't want to tell her or my dad that Brad and I talk and text all the time. My dad raised Brad, treated him like his own. Unlike his own dad, who basically disowned him.

"How was work?" I ask again, to start a new conversation thread.

She smiles at me, her first real smile of the night. "It was fine. Thanks for asking."

"Tell me something funny," I say. "We need more humour in our lives, Mom." *Plus, I need to get through this meal, and back to my room.*

She launches into a story about a couple who are both in their nineties who want to get married. They were making invitations at their craft class. We laugh, which makes the rest of dinner tolerable.

CHAPTER 3
PERFECT PDA

My alarm goes off at five in the morning and I moan. Why do swim practices have to be soooooo early? I get up, and stumble around in the dark, throwing on sweats, securing my hair in a ponytail. I stayed up until after midnight getting my lab done. I'm out the door in five minutes and at the pool in thirty. It's just a one-stop ride on the subway.

In the change room, in a sleepy daze, I yank my suit on. No one talks to me. There's this weird pecking order on the swim team, and I'm kind of low on the ladder.

I enter the pool area and immediately feel the humidity. I used to love the heat, the smell of chlorine, but lately it's been stinging my nostrils. Of course, Leo is already in the pool, doing his warm-ups. He always does extra laps, as does Jada Bhatkar, the best female swimmer on the team. I see him pop his head up. I wave, but he talks to Jada and doesn't even look over at me. Then, like fish, they go under.

I don't feel like practising, but dive in the pool anyway. It feels colder today as the water envelops me. It doesn't give me energy like it does for Leo. I do my laps, one after the other, and my legs feel like I'm dragging huge logs behind me. When I complete my laps, I get out of the pool, noticing that everyone else is standing by the coach. I'm the last one finished. Again.

I sneak to the back of the group, hoping Coach won't notice me. He doesn't. I breathe a sigh of relief. He explains the morning workout on a whiteboard, before he says, "Leo and Jada, I would like you to work on your turns together. Help each other out."

They smile at each other, and . . . do they gaze into each other's eyes too? I shake my head. It's way too early to let the green monster out of the bag. We all start moving. Then I hear Coach Maloney say, "Nova, I want to work with you on your breathing."

Heat spreads from my face to my chest. I can feel a rash developing, and it's hard to hide when you're wearing a swimsuit. I nod, unable to speak. I've been working so hard on my speed, and my breathing is just not getting me there. I glance at Leo, but he's already walking with Jada to the edge of the pool. They dive in.

Coach makes me work on my breathing in the farthest lane over, the one closest to the wall. I'm all by myself for the entire practice, doing the same thing over and over. The problem is I get partway through the lap and start gasping because of the panic in my chest.

When practice is over, I get out of the pool feeling as if I sucked. I meet up with Leo outside, and we walk to school together, holding hands. Swimming may make me tired, but walking hand in hand with Leo gives me energy.

"I took a tenth of a second off my turn," he says.

"Good for you." I can't even think in those terms. A tenth of a second?

"Felt so good, Nova. I have to get my times down for National Team tryouts."

"When are they?" I ask. I stare at the sun that's starting to peek up, and inhale a good, deep breath, enjoying my special time with Leo. The leaves on the maples are still green but soon will start turning to red, orange and yellow.

"After Christmas," he says.

I nod and swing his hand. "So happy for you."

"Thanks," he replies. We walk toward our school front doors, and when we're almost there, he says, "Jada killed hers too."

The sound of her name rolling off his tongue makes me cringe. Even I have to admit she's gorgeous, with her long, black hair and flawless brown skin. He opens the front door of the school and I walk inside. Students are milling around the lobby. Since I don't want Jada to be a part of our conversation, I stop him in the hallway and look up at him, right into his beautiful, happy eyes. "Guess what I'm doing today?" I ask coyly.

He smiles at me. I love how his eyes crinkle in the corners, how these little dimples appear in his sculpted cheeks. "You do know condoms work too," he whispers.

"Shhhh," I say, laughing. I put my fingers on his lips. Then I glance up and down the hall. No one can hear this conversation. I turn back to him, gazing into his eyes. "They can rip." His eyes stare back at me, and I could melt right here in the hall.

He tickles my stomach and I giggle. "Don't. Not here. We need to get to class." I continue laughing and squirming, enjoying every minute of him touching me, the sparks that are zapping.

He wiggles his eyebrows up and down in this funny expression he likes to do, which I think is hilarious. It's like a Groucho Marx look. "How about . . . this . . . then?"

I'm still giggling when he plants his lips on mine, kissing me, tongue and all. We push back against the concrete wall, and he puts his leg in between mine. As much as we need to get a move on, and kissing inside the school is considered PDA, I kiss him back. I don't care.

Then someone walks by us and says, "Get a room."

We break apart and I touch my tingling lips.

School is better than swim practice. I get a few early-in-the-year quizzes back, one in biology and one in physics. I pump my fists because they're both in the high nineties.

The final bell goes, and I run into Izzy as we are walking out. She falls into step beside me. "So . . . ?" she asks.

Izzy and I have this telepathic relationship, so I know exactly what she is asking. "Yeah. I'm going right now." I glance at her. "Wanna come with?"

"I wish I could. But I've got a stupid tutoring session."

"I can tutor you. Pleeeeease."

"My mom has already paid for this. She'll kill me if I miss." Izzy hip checks me. "Plus, you and I won't get anything done. We would talk other things, like sex," she whispers. "Did I tell you I'm in loooove with that new guy, Felix." She grins. "He's got the best accent."

"Yeah, okay." I shake my head at her.

She pats me on the shoulder. "Don't worry. It's easy. The appointment is seriously like five minutes."

The bus I need to take to the clinic is in the opposite direction of my apartment building. After Googling clinics, I decided to choose one farther from my home. Since I have time after school, it's no big deal to tack an extra twenty minutes on. The bus is full, so I stand. For the entire ride my knees feel as if they may buckle under me. I get off at the stop and stand in front of the brick walk-in clinic for a few seconds.

Come on, Nova, you can do this.

The door squeaks when I open it. I swear everyone turns and looks at me, knowing exactly why I'm here. I duck my head and go to the desk.

"Um," I say quietly.

"Can I help you?" The woman behind the desk is NOT talking quietly. Her voice seems to bounce off the walls.

"I'd like to see someone about, um, getting birth control."

She slides me a clipboard. "Fill this out. Is it the pill you want?"

"Um, yeah." Why does she have to be so loud?

I slink away from the desk, clipboard in hand. After I fill out the form and hand it back, she tells me to take a seat. I sit and don't look at anyone. What if someone from my mother's work is here? Or someone from her opinionated book club. They're always in these deep religious and political discussions. I clasp my hands in my lap and stare at them. The vinyl chair feels hard. The room stuffy. A woman keeps clearing her throat. So gross. Why doesn't she just go to the restroom, already?

Finally, my name is called. I'm ushered into a room, and again I sit and wait. I'm not sure why I'm feeling this anxiety, but I am. I stare at the bed with the crinkly paper. What if the doctor wants to do a pap test? What if that same doctor is male? My heart is still pounding against my jacket when the door opens. A Black woman walks in and smiles at me. A genuine smile. Immediately, I relax.

"I'm Dr. Robinson," she says. "What can I do for you today?"

The appointment takes all of ten minutes. She asks me if I've had sex. I say no. She tells me I was smart to come in and get the pill before having sex. I'm being responsible. But, in all fairness, that is basically my middle name. I've always been the responsible one. Prescription in hand, I walk outside.

CHAPTER 4
EARLY AND LATE

"What did you want to tell me that's so important?" Izzy asks. "Your text was mysterious. We are in first-period Biology together and she sits directly behind me.

I'm facing her because class hasn't started yet, otherwise I'd face front and listen. I lean across her desk because god help me if anyone hears what I'm about to say, especially the guys. "My period came early," I whisper. "I started the pill."

She squeals. And does this hand-clapping thingy. "The big day is coming." She sings her words. "And it's about time." She puts her hands up and I high-five them.

I glance around again, and I do see that we're surrounded by other students, lots of guys, those who might want to listen to our conversation. If the guys hear they'll start the comments flying like, "Nova's gonna be a bitch today."

I whisper, "I got my period out of the blue again. In the middle of the month, so I was able to start the pill earlier than I thought."

"No waiting for you!" Izzy laughs, then glances around too. She turns back to me and whispers. "You and your wacky periods."

"Yeah, well, swimming."

She shakes her head. "You and that sport."

"Swimming is becoming a grind," I say in a normal voice.

"Last night I was up until midnight. When my alarm went off this morning, I thought I was going to die. All I wanted to do was sleep. I think I might quit."

Izzy scrunches up her face. "I'll never for a million years — no make that a gazillion — understand why you subject yourself to such punishment."

"It's okay." I shrug. But has it been lately? I've been dreading the water every practice since we started up at the beginning of the school year. Something is missing. If I was to be honest with myself, I hate swimming right now.

Izzy glances over my shoulder. Her eyes go wide. "Here comes Felix. Man, he's hot. I swear, Nova, I'm doing him before we graduate from this joint."

"*Doing him?*" I shake my head. "Okay, that's disgusting."

"Okay, then, I'm going to *make love* to him." She playfully smirks.

"You in love. Now it's my turn to say . . . yeah, right."

The teacher starts talking, so I turn around to face the front. *Make love.* That's what I want to do with Leo. The reason why I've been waiting.

* * *

At lunch, I meet up with Leo in the cafeteria. He always has people who want to sit with him, including Jada. He's popular because he's the best swimmer in our school, and in the entire city of Toronto, possibly soon to be one of the best in all of Canada. When he sees me, he stands, and gives me a wave. I wave back and make my way to his table. He makes room for me, right beside him. Our thighs touch. He puts his arm around me, and I lean into him. God, he feels good.

"I can't wait for our swim meet," says Jada. She's sitting across from us.

"I'm with you," says Leo.

"This year we need to be the number one school in Toronto." Jada loves her swim team talk, which is all she talks about. I swear she has flippers for feet, she's that fast. And Leo has an arm span that makes recruiters drool.

Leo nods. "We're going to kick butt."

Something sinks inside of me. I'm not the one who will get our swim team any points. I never win any individual races, so my only help can possibly be with the relay team. I move closer to Leo and put my hand on his thigh. Jada only looks at Leo, not me. There's a weird vibe going off between them and it bugs me. I want to tell her, "He's mine," but I guess that's why I'm touching him. I inch my fingers up his thigh. He shifts closer to me.

"What did everyone think about the English assignment?" I ask. Maybe a little too loudly. I wish I could take my words back, make them softer or something. Both Jada and Leo have English this semester as well, with the same teacher that I have.

They both look at me like I have horns coming out the top of my head. My detouring of the conversation is probably a little obvious, but since I've started, I continue. Speaking in a much quieter voice, I say, "I love the novel that's been chosen." And I do, that's a fact. "*The Agony of Bun O'Keefe* sounds as if it has so many layers. I'm looking forward to our discussions in class."

Jada's gaze immediately shifts from me to Leo. She flings that long, silky black hair of hers as she snaps her fingers. She's the only swimmer I know who has hair that doesn't look like straw. "I forgot to tell you, Leo." She speaks quickly as if what she has to say is more important than what I just said. "Marc, from Central, has a shoulder injury. Might need surgery."

"Wow," says Leo. "That sucks for him."

I touch the ends of my dry hair, sit tall and try not to feel offended that they are not interested in discussing something other than swimming. Right now, I hate swimming even more than I did before.

"That's not a worry for you, though," says Jada. She gives Leo this weird, kind of sexy smile. "His times don't come close to yours."

Leo gives a little shrug. "He's decent at the backstroke."

"Yeah, but we cut time off our turns today." She almost sings her words. Then she holds up her hands and Leo taps them.

Beside him I sink. Since I don't really know this Marc guy, except that he's a good swimmer, I can't add to this conversation. I listen to them go back and forth about "Marc" for a few minutes before I stand up.

"I'm going to get some fries," I say. "Anyone want anything?"

Jada holds up her hand. "Not for me, thanks. You never know what's in cafeteria food."

Although I want to say something nasty to her, I don't. She's got, like, zero per cent body fat because all she eats is quinoa and lettuce. I smile instead. "Too bad," I say. "They make good fries. And the gravy is even better."

I take a step to leave the table, but then Leo stands too. "I'll go with you," he says.

As we walk toward the food stations, he slings his arm around me. "How come your hair never smells like chlorine?" he whispers. "And always smells sexy, like exotic mangos."

"Must be my shampoo," I say, snuggling into him. He pulls me closer and kisses my hair as we walk. I sneak a quick glance over at Jada, and she's staring at us, so I squeeze his butt just so she can see.

* * *

The alarm keeps chiming. I grab my phone and look at the time. Holy crap. I jump out of bed, my head pounding. That social essay last night had me working until two. I'm late. So late. Crap. Crap. Crap.

The morning air is nippy. Fall is on its way, winter and snow coming. I yank the collar of my jacket up and run down the sidewalk, my feet slapping the concrete. The black sky and cool fall air make me want to go back home and dive under my duvet. But I keep running, my bag crashing against my legs. I just miss a subway train and groan. Poor timing. I lean against the wall as I wait for the next one, continually glancing at my phone to see the minutes ticking by.

I'm huffing and puffing when I get to the pool. No one is in the pool change room when I fling open the door. Yeah, I'm late. I quickly get changed, shove my hair under my swim cap and strap my goggles on. I head out to the pool, and everyone is swimming their warm-up laps. Coach Maloney glances over at me and gives me a dirty look.

"Nice of you to show up, Nova."

"Sorry," I mumble. I dive in the water.

I've only done two laps when the whistle blows. I gather around with everyone else.

"Nova," says our coach. "Finish your warm-up."

I see Leo shake his head in obvious disappointment. I shrink inside and slither back into the pool. By the time I'm done my warm-up, the others are well into their workout.

In the last half hour of the practice, Coach Maloney puts another swimmer in my spot on the relay team, and I get to sit on the sidelines and shiver.

* * *

"What's the matter?" Izzy asks in Math class. She's dolled up more than she dolls up, wearing a little makeup, and a skirt and booties. I'm wearing jeans and a sweatshirt, my usual after-swim-practice attire.

"I was late for swimming today," I moan. Coach Maloney made me look like an idiot. He took me off the relay team and the new team had a faster time. In other words, I suck."

"That does suck," says Izzy. "Mr. Maloney is good at making people look like idiots. I was late for his History class once and he totally embarrassed me."

"I'm seriously thinking . . ." I tap my pencil on my notebook. ". . . especially after this morning, that I should . . . quit swimming." I've thought this before but never said it out loud.

"You know my answer to that," says Izzy. "Who the hell wants to get up at five thirty every morning to jump in cold water? I mean, seriously. Especially if you hate it. What are you, a masochist?"

"For me, it's more about my schoolwork."

"Yeah, right."

"What's that supposed to mean?"

She rolls her eyes at me. "The only reason you stay on the team is to spend time with Leo and keep an eye on him."

I make a funny face at her. "Who made you my psychologist?" She has a bit of a point. When I'm on the team, we get to travel together, eat meals with the team. I sometimes get to sit with him on the bus.

"Admit it. I'm right," she says.

"Sort of, but not really. It's not to keep an eye on him but to be *with him.*"

"Again, I call B.S. on that."

"Okay, okay. I do like to intervene now and again."

"I've got a solution for you."

"And what would that be?"

She leans forward and whispers. "Sex. Then he'll always want to be with *you*! I guarantee you'll see shooting stars! And he'll see more than stars!"

"Shooting stars." I laugh. "Okay, sure."

Suddenly, it hits me. I forgot to take my pill in my rush to get to swim practice. Oh well, no worries, Leo and I haven't come to that yet. I wonder when our magical moment will be. I smile to myself, loving having these exciting thoughts skipping through my brain.

CHAPTER 5
HURTFUL COMMENTS

For some reason — well, I know the reason — I don't get up the nerve to quit the swim team ASAP. The reason is Jada. She follows Leo like a puppy dog, and he seems to lap her attention up like water. Izzy is right, if I'm still on the team, I can keep an eye on things.

But then I get a low ninety on a test. And I get an eight out of ten on a lab.

And . . . I miss my alarm again.

I'm sitting in the change room, half dressed, hair wet after swim practice, so tired I can hardly move to put on my clothes. Jada looks at me from across the room and gives me this disgusted look. Then she turns her back on me and starts brushing that stunning hair of hers with some pink brush that seems to shine under the fluorescent lights. The other girls on the team seem to be mad at me too. Okay, I was late again. And we have a meet coming up. And Coach Maloney did make me sit again. I'm still off the relay team. No one is talking to me, and whispers are happening behind my back.

I'm not being a good teammate. I sit on the hard change room bench and lean against the wall. I close my eyes. What am I going to do? I hate the swim team right now and Izzy is right, if it wasn't for Leo, I'd quit. My exhausted body doesn't want to move until I hear my phone buzz.

I pull it out. Text from Leo. Is he going to be mad at me too?

Can't wait for your bday. Big plans.

I smile. Why do I keep torturing myself? I talked to him about maybe quitting swimming over the weekend and he didn't seem to care. I glance across the room and see Jada, who is now finished brushing her hair, stuffing her legs into jeans that are probably two sizes smaller than mine. Her body is the perfect athlete's build: lean, muscular. I look at my phone again, and smile at the text. He texted me and not her, so what am I worried about? Leo doesn't care if I'm a good swimmer, he wants to do something special for *my* birthday. And he always tells me he *loves my body*. I grin and text back.

What? What?

Haha. No surprise if I tell you!

After I stuff my phone back in my bag, still grinning, I finish getting dressed. Now I really don't care that no one is talking to me. Jada is talking nonstop about swimming to everyone but me, but she's talking loud enough that I think she wants me to hear.

Today is a tights and long T-shirt day. I get dressed and head out to meet Leo so we can walk hand in hand to school. Leo and I arrive a bit late, so after a peck on the cheek we go our separate ways for our classes. Just as I'm rounding a corner, rushing to get to math for a quiz, I run into Coach Maloney.

"Nova. Slow down."

"I have a math quiz, Mr. Maloney. That's the reason I was late this morning. I'm so sorry."

He stops in front of me even though I do have to keep moving. "Don't let it happen again," he says.

I think of Leo's text. How he still wants me if I'm not on the stupid swim team and suddenly, I just blurt out, "Mr. Maloney, I think I need to quit."

"Okay, Nova. Any reason why?" He crosses his arms, putting his hands under his armpits.

I inhale to get some courage. I've started this now and it's time to finish. "I . . . I . . . I don't think I can, uh, manage the practices anymore. I'm not swimming next year, and I want to go to a top-notch medical school after my undergrad. I need good marks." I pause. "It's just hard to be a quitter."

"Nova, I do understand. As far as I'm concerned, you're quitting for all the right reasons. It seems to me you may have thought this through. And you have your priorities straight. And to be on my team, I need commitment, which lately you haven't been giving."

I look at the toe of my sneaker. The dirty floor. "I'm sorry," I say.

Coach Maloney puts his hand on my shoulder. "We'll miss you."

I finally smile. "Thanks, Mr. Maloney."

He smiles back and pushes his glasses up his nose. "You better get to class."

Once I'm away from Coach Maloney, I check my phone. I have thirty seconds to get to my desk. As I'm speeding down the hall, Jada catches up with me. "What was that all about?" I glance at her. Did she follow me out of the pool?

I don't want to tell her before I tell Leo, so I keep my fast clip going, my legs pushing me forward. My backpack slaps against my back. "Nothing, really. I need to hurry. Math quiz first period."

"Let's talk at lunch," she says.

Let's not, I think.

After my quiz, which I think I aced, I text Leo. I need to let him know ASAP about what went down with Mr. Maloney. I don't want him to hear this from someone else. Especially Jada.

Meet me outside cafeteria.

He texts back with a checkmark emoji.

He's waiting for me at the door of the cafeteria, and just the sight of him makes my heart flutter. When he sees me, he hugs me, and I put my head on his chest. He kisses the top of my head. "What's up?"

"I have something to tell you." I look up at him. "I want to tell you first before everyone else finds out."

"I could kiss you right here in the hall," he says, his eyes twinkling.

"Be serious." I put my hand on his chest.

"Okay. What's going on?"

"I quit."

"Quit what? Sure hoping you're not quitting on me, cuz I got birthday plans, baby."

"Not you." I playfully punch his chest. "The swim team."

He more or less rolls his eyes. The guy version of what Izzy does to me when I'm over-the-top dramatic. So it's more of a side look. "Oh, that again," he mumbles. "No biggie. I might have quit if I were you too."

"What's that supposed to mean?" I back away from him.

He laughs and pulls me over to him again. "You're not getting away from me." He nuzzles his nose in my hair. "It means . . . damn, you smell good."

"Leo!" I push away from him but just a little bit. "What did you mean?"

"Nothing. Come here. Give me a kiss before we have to get back to class."

A teacher walks by us, coughs and says, "Hallways are for walking."

We hold hands going down the hall and split at the corner. All the way to my next class I think about what he said. He's right. I'm not the best swimmer . . . but did he have to say it like that? A part of me is hurt.

The usual gang meets for lunch, and I ask Izzy to join us, but she's going somewhere with Felix. Where? I have no idea. But somewhere in her car. She is all smiles and then some.

Cold pizza is all I could find in the fridge this morning. I've had one bite when Jada asks, "So what did Coach Maloney want?"

I'm about to say "none of your business" when Leo says, "Nova quit the swim team." He puts his arm around me and squeezes my upper arm.

"Oh," says Jada. She shrugs. "About time."

"Excuse me?" I glare at her.

Leo laughs. "She doesn't mean anything by it. It's not like it's going to hurt us getting that overall trophy."

"Thanks," I mutter. I lower my head and eat my pizza.

CHAPTER 6
BIRTHDAY SURPRISE

My birthday has always fallen in that first month of going back to school — September 30. In elementary school, it was okay because everyone looked forward to a birthday party. But since high school started it falls in that we've-been-in-school-for-almost-four-weeks-now-so-let's-pile-on-the-work time. Teachers start giving out the midterm schedule just when it hits. This comes with intensity in senior year. Those early fall grades count toward university acceptance.

I wake up on my birthday to the smell of baking. And no alarm. I look at my clock and when I see it is seven, I sink into my mattress and pull my duvet up to my chin. I want to just lie still for a few minutes and do nothing. I don't have to jump out of bed to jump in a cold pool. I close my eyes and breathe. What a great feeling. I think about tonight, and how Leo wants to do something special for my birthday and has been going on and on about how it's a big surprise. And it's on a Friday too!

After a few seconds of being happy and contented under the covers, I do get up and head out to the kitchen. Mom is peeling the wrapper off a package of cream cheese. The bowl of icing sugar sits on the small kitchen counter.

She sees me and smiles. "Happy Birthday, honey!"

"Thanks," I say. I push tangled hair off my face. "Smells great in here! You're baking early."

"I have to work, so I thought I would get it done. Your birthday carrot cake." She drops the cream cheese into the sugar. "What do you want for your birthday meal?" She seems upbeat, which is a bit of a change.

"Leo wants to take me out tonight," I say.

"Oh," she says. "Okay. Where are you two going?"

"I'm not sure. He's keeping it a surprise." I see that the coffee pot is full, so I grab a mug from the cupboard. "We can do dinner tomorrow."

"Of course." She doesn't look at me. "I think your dad might even be home tomorrow."

"Is he still sleeping?"

"No. He had an early-morning shift, so he's already gone." She turns to me and gives me a halfhearted smile. "He said to say happy birthday and he'll see you later today."

"He's sure logging the hours," I say. "I wanted to tell him I quit the swim team."

"I told him."

"Oh, okay. I wanted to tell him."

"He's okay with it," she says. "He's got his own worries right now."

With a mug of coffee in hand, I go to my room to get dressed. I rifle through my closet. It's a jeans and pretty blouse or sweater day. I want to look half decent on my birthday. As I'm pushing hangers I think about tonight. What should I wear? I still don't even know what he has planned. I push hanger after hanger until suddenly I stop.

Enough. I can't stress about what I'm wearing *tonight*, because I need to get to school now.

* * *

Izzy meets me at the front door of the school, holding a balloon. How embarrassing.

"Seriously, Izzy," I say laughing. "Now the whole school will know."

"That's the plan."

"Can I pop it?"

She yanks it away from me. "No, you can't pop it. I'm tying it to your locker."

We walk into the school, our strides matching. She bumps me with her shoulder. "Speaking of plans. I have one for after school. I know what I want to get you for your birthday."

"You don't have to get me anything."

She winks at me. "Oh, but I do."

* * *

We hit Yorkdale Mall after school, which is early afternoon because we both have spares last class on Friday. Leo is at a training session for his club swimming team, but has told me he is coming to pick me up for my birthday surprise at seven. First, Izzy buys me a special coffee. "You will need this," she says.

"It might not happen."

She nods. "Oh, I think it might. It's on the birthday schedule."

"Honestly? Have you been working with Leo on this birthday present?"

She grins. "Maybe a little."

I sip my latte as we walk down the halls of the mall, heading toward what store, I have no idea. "It sounds so contrived," I say. "Isn't something like this supposed to be organic? I don't want this to be put on a schedule."

"Don't worry." She stops walking. "Here's the store, my friend."

I glance up and see that the store is Victoria's Secret, a lingerie-slash-pajama store.

"You need new undies, birthday girl. Granny panties don't cut it."

I laugh. But a part of me is glad that she thought about this. I do have a drawer full of stretched-out undies and bras. Buying lingerie with my hard-earned tutor money just doesn't seem like a responsible thing to do. We enter the store and she holds up a lacy red bra. "This is it!" She laughs. "This is the one!"

"Ohmygod. Are you kidding me?"

She slaps her legs, howling in laughter. "Yes. I'm kidding," she says. "You think I don't know that you wouldn't be caught dead in *red* lingerie." She pulls on my jean jacket. "Come on. Let's go find the *beige* ones. With no lace and no frills."

"You got that right," I say.

She hands me three sets and sends me to the change room. The first two are a disaster. One is huge. And my boobs are spilling out everywhere in the other one. I've got the third beige bra and underwear set on when Izzy knocks on the door.

"Let me see that one," she says.

I open the door a crack and give her a quick look. I've done this for the last two.

She looks me up and down and says, "Looking hot." She puts her finger to her lips and does a sizzling sound.

"Oh, stop." I laugh and shut the door in her face.

From the other side she says, "That's the one!"

I take it off and put my clothes back on. I check my phone and see that Leo texted. I want to take a photo of the underwear and send it to him, but I don't. We're not into that kind of stuff. He's worried about someone finding it and sending it to his college recruiter. I'll just model it tonight if we get to that moment.

I exhale. I put my hand to my chest and exhale. This could be the night I've been waiting for. I step out of the change room and Izzy holds up her phone.

"That seriously took less than fifteen minutes to outfit you."

"Simple gets the job done."

Izzy takes the set from my hands. "Gotta wear what you feel comfortable in," she says. "Plus, it's on sale. Half price. I'm liking that action."

"Let's split it," I say.

"Not a chance."

We head to the counter and she pulls out her wallet. I do too and find a twenty. I try to give it to her, but she pushes my arm away. "Nope. This is your birthday gift." Then she grins. "Oh, and Christmas too."

We leave with me holding on to a little pink-and-black bag. And my heart racing in my chest, like it might explode and leave me completely breathless.

Is that what's going to happen tonight?

Shooting stars!

CHAPTER 7
CANDLES AND COVERS

Leo has his arm around me as we walk toward the Yonge subway station. He just picked me up at my apartment because he said he wanted us to be on a real date. I'm impressed. So was my dad. We pass by the fire station, and the church, with the night air circling us. I feel as if I'm in a bubble, and there's only the two of us inside it. The rest of the world is outside of us, unable to do any harm. I lean into him. If I were a cat, I would purr loudly. I feel so content snuggled up against him.

"Where are we going?" I ask, using the sexiest voice I can muster.

"You'll see." He kisses the top of my head.

We get on the subway train and stand. He leans into me and says, "We're two stops away." I inhale again, taking in his masculine scent.

I think about what he has just said. Two stops? The station I always get off at to get to his house is just two stops. I think of restaurants around that area and there are a few, but we certainly won't be in the hub of downtown, on King Street where all the funky restaurants are, like Laissez Faire. That was the one I was hoping for.

The doors of the subway fly open and we get off. We walk hand in hand the few blocks through his neighbourhood. We must be going to his house. When we don't go down his street I'm confused, but then we turn when we hit his back alley. I'm not sure why we are going down the back alley, but I follow Leo's lead. His house is the third one down, and he creaks open the back gate. As we are heading down the stone walkway, toward the patio and back door, I notice immediately that all the lights are off.

"My parents are away," he says, as if reading my mind.

"Like, out of town?" My hands start shaking a little. Does this mean what I think it means?

"Oh, yeah." He takes my hand and kisses the back of it. Then he starts singing, "*All night long. All night long.*"

I burst out laughing at his singing. He grabs me and spins me around.

"Let's waltz," he says.

"Leoooo!" I laugh so hard I feel as if I'm going to pee my pants. Leo waltzing is like an octopus dancing in a hot frying pan. All limbs going everywhere.

Totally out of sync, we stumble into each other. I'm still laughing hysterically when he pulls me into him and kisses me right there in the backyard. Under the night sky, stars shining down, I kiss him back.

When we pull apart, he says, "Come on, let's go inside." He sounds excited.

Holding my hand, Leo walks me up the porch and through the back entrance, which leads to the kitchen. He doesn't turn on any lights. The kitchen smells amazing, like someone has been cooking with garlic. He takes my coat and hangs it up.

Then he says, "Wait here."

I stand in the dark, but with the streetlights shining through the French doors, I can see shapes, like the pots on the stove. And the bread beside the stovetop, ready to go in the oven. I hear a flicking sound. Then I see a flash of light twinkle through the dark. Leo comes back into the kitchen and slides across the hardwood in his sock feet to get to me. He pulls me in his arms and kisses me again, long and deep, his hands running up and down my spine.

Then he takes my hand and guides me to the dining room. My eyes widen and I put my hand to my chest in awe. The table is set with his mother's good dishes, wineglasses included. Four candles shine bright. He even has a wine bucket beside the table. A little present bag sits beside one of the plates.

"Oh, Leo. This is so perfect," I say.

"I looked up how to set the table online," he says. "The wine bucket was my idea, though. Although it's for white wine and we have red. But it looks good, right?" He laughs.

I laugh along with him. "Looks fantastic. I glance around again at what he's done. "I'm impressed. This is . . . so . . . sophisticated." I clasp my hands together. He did this for me.

He did this for me.

"Sit down." He pulls out my chair, bowing at the waist. "My laaaady."

His playfulness makes me giggle. He leaves, and I hear pots banging and a few swear words come out of the kitchen. I keep giggling. "Can I help?" I call out.

"Nope, I got this."

"Okay." I smile behind my hand. I feel like a princess, sitting in wait. No one waits on me anymore.

Seconds later, he brings out a bottle of wine. "Not sure what kind this is," he says, "but I stole it from my parents' stash downstairs. They'll never know. It's one of the ones my dad says is crap anyway."

He unscrews the top on the wine and pours us both a glass. He sits down. "Cheers," he says.

I clink his glass back. "This is so sweet of you, Leo. You've gone to so much trouble," I say. Inside, my heart is growing until I feel it might burst open.

"Not really," he says. "The spaghetti sauce is from a jar. I looked up how to make it online. It would have taken days to make it homemade. So many ingredients. Plus, I didn't actually know half of the stuff."

I laugh. "It'll be great." I sip the wine. It tastes fine to me.

"Open your present," he says.

First, I pull the wrinkled tissue out of the bag. I love how it's been stuffed in there. Then I feel in the bottom of the bag and find a little box. When I've got the lid off the box, I see a pretty, silver necklace with a starfish on it.

"Ohmygod, I love it," I say. And I do. He knows I love starfish.

"I got it at American Eagle," he says.

"I want to put it on."

He stands up and walks behind me, pulling my hair back. He kisses my neck first before helping clasp up the necklace. Then he drops his hands, so they are touching my breasts. He leaves them there, just hanging, barely touching. "I can't wait for later," he whispers in my ear.

"Same," I whisper back. My heart picks up its pace. My throat dries. His hands start to move, making circles, massaging my breasts. A moaning sound escapes my mouth.

"We could always eat dinner after." His warm breath tickles my ear. He smells so good. The touch of his lips against my skin make me go all mushy inside. A ball of something gets caught in my throat and I can't answer. I nod instead. And stand. Why wait?

He turns me toward him and gently puts his hands on my face. "I've been waiting for this night."

"Me too," I say.

He takes my hand and leads me to his bedroom. His bed is made but he has the sheets pulled back just like in a hotel room. And he doesn't have a basketball duvet, but a plain navy one. He's thought of everything. I'm flattered. And excited. And nervous too. All of the above.

"Let's keep the lights off," I say.

He flicks the switch. The room darkens.

We lay down on the bed, and in seconds we are kissing, and touching each other everywhere. Everything seems to build so fast. It's like a frenzy. Our clothes come off next and are tossed to the floor. He unclasps my bra and tosses it too. So much for the birthday gift Izzy got me. He didn't even see it. I didn't get to model it.

Leo tries to put on a condom, but it rips. "Crap," he says. "That's never happened before."

What he means by "that has never happened before," I don't want to know.

"You're on the pill, right?" he asks quickly.

"Yeah," I whisper.

He pulls me under the covers. I'm naked. Completely naked. I'm glad to be underneath something. I can feel the heat from his body next to mine.

"You're so beautiful," he whispers. His hands touch me everywhere. My hip bones, my thighs, my breasts. And in between. Yes, in between.

Funny, I don't feel beautiful. I just feel weird. Like I'm having an out-of-body experience. I don't have a clue what I'm doing.

"Are you okay?" he whispers. "We can stop."

"I'm good," I whisper.

After more kissing, and more touching, it happens.

It. Happens.

There are moments I like. But the truth is, it hurts a little. And didn't exactly feel like I thought it would. Maybe I just need practice.

Leo collapses on top of me and my hair gets caught under his arm. I don't want to say anything because he is breathing like he just swam a race. Then he rolls off me. I yank the sheets up until they are under my chin. He puts his arm around me, pulling me into him.

"That was incredible. You're incredible." He runs his finger down my cheek. My body relaxes and I snuggle into him. This part I like better than the other part. My body curves to fit his, and I like how the heat from his body radiates into mine.

A little sliver of a light shines through his bedroom window. I stare out, and I see the half moon.

But then a huge cloud passes over it and it disappears, covering the shooting stars.

CHAPTER 8
PRACTICE MAKES PERFECT

"Give me the goods," says Izzy the next day.

I'm at Izzy's, hanging out. My mother was asking too many questions about my night, and I had to get out of the apartment before I spewed more lies. Izzy's bedroom is a mess, with every available space filled. Clothes are strewn everywhere. Water glasses sit on her nightstand. Shoes are toppled on the floor like she just stepped out of them. Yup, we're different. But she's the one I want to talk to.

"It was great," I say with a bit too much enthusiasm. The night flashes through my mind. It was a great night, except for the actual sex part. We drank the wine and ate the pasta wrapped in his bed sheets. That was fun. And we laughed about all kinds of stupid stuff as we got a little tipsy. Leo even went downstairs and got another bottle of wine, and then we got into a few shots of some creamy drink. I got home after midnight and my mother was waiting. Of course, she leaned in close to smell my breath. Leo and I showered together so I wouldn't smell like sex when I got home. That was fun too. Although the sex in the shower didn't work like it does in the movies. My back got a bit scratched from the shower nozzle.

"Okay, that's so not sounding *great*." Her knitting needles are clacking away.

"Honestly, I liked the before and after better." I liked laying together. Cuddling. Feeling skin against skin. "I think . . . I need experience, practice." I'm also sore, chafed and red, but I don't want to tell Izzy that.

"That's to be expected," says Izzy.

I pick up a pillow off the floor and throw it at her. She dodges it. "Hey, that will throw off my row." She holds up her knitting. "These socks are going to keep someone warm this winter. I don't want them to be lopsided."

"You said shooting stars," I say.

She stops knitting and turns to me. "Okay, so they sputtered a bit. Give them time."

"Do you see stars with Felix?"

"I see everything with Felix. But . . ." Izzy pauses, and I wait for the "but" to continue.

"But . . . I want to wait with him," she says. "We haven't gone there yet. I don't know, Nova, he's different. I really like him. And I want this one to be special. Not some flippant deal in some random bedroom or car."

"Holy crap."

She bites her bottom lip. I see a dreamy sort of look on her face.

"Are you in love?" I ask.

"Not love yet. That's for sure. But I'm definitely in big-time something." Izzy leans her head back and closes her eyes. "I just get all tingly and mushy when I'm near him. No one has even done that to me before."

I think about Leo. I'm like that with him, every time he's near me, every single time he touches me. So why was the actual sex part so much of a disappointment?

"I feel like that with Leo too," I say. "Maybe I just need more practice."

"Practice pays off," she says. "You have to relax your body when you've having sex. Enjoy it."

"Okay. I'll try."

"What time did you get home?"

"Late. My mom was like a snapping turtle when I walked in. Question after question." I laugh. "It's hard to lie about being in a restaurant for over five hours."

Izzy laughs. "What'd you tell her?"

"Oh, the standard, we went to the Beaches and sat looking out at Lake Ontario, enjoying the fall air, and beautiful view and blah, blah, blah."

"Meanwhile you were copulating under bed covers. How'd the underwear fly?"

"After it was tossed on the floor, I modelled it. It was well received. So, thanks! Much appreciated."

"Anytime." She winks at me. Then she goes back to her clicking needles.

Just as she says that my phone goes off. I look at my screen and see Leo's name. I quickly answer.

"Hey," I say.

"I just finished swimming," he says. "But my parents are still gone, so some of us are meeting at my house for a movie night. Nothing too crazy." I hear voices in the background. I try to figure out who they are, but they're muffled.

"Okay," I say. "Can Izzy come?"

Izzy shakes her head at me. Then she mouths, "It's fine."

"Sure," says Leo.

"Okay, see ya soon." I press End. "Come," I say to Izzy. "It's just a movie night at Leo's."

"Who's gonna be there?"

I shrug. "I dunno. Probably some of the swimmers who are on

his club team. Ask Felix to come too — I'm sure Leo won't mind. I'll text and see if we can bring one more body."

I manage to convince Izzy to text Felix and he agrees right away. So I text Leo, and he says fine but don't tell anyone else. He doesn't want a party.

When we hook up with Felix, at the corner of Yonge and Davisville, he seems thrilled to be going to a *house party*, being invited somewhere, anywhere.

"Let's walk," says Izzy, linking her arm in his. "It's not that far."

"Sure," he says. "In London, all we do is walk."

As we head in the direction of Leo's I ask, "Do you ever get to see the queen?"

He laughs and launches into a tirade about the royal family. It's a perfect fall night, and I enjoy listening to his London stories. The leaves have just started to turn colour, a few are falling and the temperature hovers above zero. Stars blink above us. I don't talk much. Felix continues with his stories, which I find interesting and funny. We end up laughing a lot. Izzy does seem taken with the guy, and I can see why. With each step, I look forward to seeing Leo.

Leo answers the door and right away gives me a hug. I curve into his arms, like I'm a big piece of putty wanting to be moulded. He kisses the top of my head before he lets me go. "Everyone's downstairs. We've got pizza coming soon."

We head downstairs and "everyone" is only six people. Jada is sitting near the end of the sofa, and as soon as she sees me, she jumps up. "Hey, Nova. I'm sure you'll want to sit by Leo."

Um, yeah, ya think? He is my boyfriend. And we did have sex last night.

The movie is one of the *Star Wars* episodes. I'm so-so into *Star Wars*, but they are Leo's favourites. And apparently Jada's too. I sit down beside Leo, in the spot Jada was in. Jada perches beside me on the end of the sofa, which is annoying. They talk nonstop over me about all the characters and movies. When the pizza comes, I offer to go upstairs and answer the door. After I hand over the money, I carry the pizza boxes downstairs. Jada has taken my spot on the sofa.

Izzy comes up beside me and whispers, "He's *your* boyfriend." This makes me feel better that I'm not the only one noticing that Jada's trying to move in on Leo.

I nod and plunk the pizza on the coffee table. Once I have my slice I sit on the floor, in front of Leo. I put my body between his legs, so we are touching.

The evening ends at eleven. I say goodbye to Felix and Izzy at the door. Izzy leans into me and whispers. "You staying here?"

I nod. Then I whisper. "My mom thinks I'm sleeping at your place. Help me out here."

"I got your back." She holds up her thumb.

"Thanks." I give her a hug.

The door shuts and it's just me and Leo and Jada.

"Your parents are, *for sure*, gone tonight?" I ask him, touching his face, knowing Jada is watching. Also wanting her to know I'm *staying overnight.*

He pulls me into his arms. "They're gone. No worries."

Keys jingling make us turn around. Leo lets go of me.

"See you at school," I say to Jada.

"Yeah, I'm going to head too," says Jada. She glances quickly at me, before she smiles at Leo. "I'll swing by and pick you up in the morning for practice. I've got the car."

"Sure," he says. "That'd be great."

"Don't you have your parents' car?" I ask. As soon as I say this, I wish I could take it back because my words came out like a whiny, jealous girlfriend.

Leo rolls his eyes. "They take the keys. Don't want me driving when they're gone."

"We carpool all the time," says Jada in this stupid chipper voice.

She leaves and I'm the one who shuts the door behind her.

* * *

I wake up in a strange bed. Light streaming through a window. And I'm snuggled under a navy duvet cover. Mine is purple with yellow flowers. Right. It's Leo's. But there's no Leo. When I look at my phone, I see it's already eight thirty. I sit up. I have a text message from Leo saying he didn't want to wake me, and he's gone to his club swimming practice. Jeepers. Why didn't I wake up?

Then I remember that it was Jada who was picking him up. She probably brought him some healthy smoothie too. My insides sour, just thinking of her greeting him with her smile and smoothie. Then them driving in the car together, talking about *Star Wars* or bloody swimming.

On the floor beside the bed, I see my rumpled clothes. We were in a hurry to get everything shed last night. I get dressed right away, feeling super uncomfortable in his bedroom, his house, without him. I want a shower, clean clothes, especially clean underwear, but I'll wait until I get home. I make his bed, running my hands over it again and again, making sure there are no creases. Then I fluff up the pillow one last time before looking at myself in the mirror. My hair is a mess of tangles and my face looks a little raw from all our kissing. I glance around for a brush or comb, and see one sitting on Leo's dresser, only it's pink, and looks a lot like that one Jada uses. I shake my head. It's a brush.

53

Probably bought at Shoppers Drug Mart. His mother could have the same one. I pick it up and see a strand of dark hair in the brush. His mother is blond.

My stomach lurches.

My hands shaking, I put the brush down. I have to get out of here.

I creak open the door, and peer down the hall. What if his parents decide to come home early? How would I even talk to them now? The hall is empty, the house quiet. I tiptoe out and listen carefully for voices. I don't hear anything but white noise. Every sound is amplified, the fridge running sounds like a cement truck revving its engine. Now my head is throbbing. All I can see is that brush.

I sprint down the hall to the bathroom and quickly shut the door. I lean against it and blow out air. I feel sick. I throw up in the toilet. My body trembling, I clean up my mouth with a hand towel, then I stare at myself in the mirror. Who is looking back at me? We had sex. And now I find this out! I touch the skin on my face again, running my fingers over the raw patches. I need to go home. I creak open the bathroom door and stare up and down the hall. When I don't hear any sounds, I head to the stairs leading down to the living room. One step at a time, I gingerly make my way down, keeping my ears attuned for those voices I don't want to hear. None. I move through the living room and dining room, the place where Leo made me such a great birthday meal. My birthday meal. Which he took such care to make. For me. A pain stabs my heart.

I gather my coat and backpack, and rush outside, making sure the door is locked behind me. I scurry down the back alley, trying to make myself as small as a mouse. God, I feel as if I'm doing the walk of shame.

The subway on Sunday morning is empty. No commuters. I plunk down in a seat and exhale. Then it hits me. Crap. Crap. Crap. I yank my backpack to my lap and start searching through it. Then I shake my head. Of course, I wouldn't have my pills in here. I went to the party from Izzy's. I have to remember to take them when I get home.

As the subway wheels roll, I think about the night. We made love three times. Three times! He kept wanting more and more. And because I'm on the pill, Leo loved just rolling over instead of fussing with a condom.

He did it with me. Not Jada! But does he do it with her too? Was I good? Is she better? I run my finger down the streetcar window. Jada went home. She knew I was staying. Could I just be making a big deal about this? Maybe in their carpooling she left that brush in his car? That's a logical explanation. Right? *Right, Nova?*

After all, he kept saying how fantastic I was. Me. He said I was. Not her. The sex was so much better. I thought I was more relaxed. He made love to me. To me.

Not her. Not her. Not her.

After all my waiting and buildup and wanting the guy I'm desperately in love with . . . I don't want to even think that he could be *doing it* with both of us at the same time.

PART TWO

MAY 9

"Nova, slow down," says Brad. *"Take a big breath and exhale."*

I do what he says, but it doesn't help. It feels as if I can't get any air to my lungs. My chest heaves, up and down. I gasp for breath. I can still see blood in front of me, staring at me, on the walls, the floor, almost as if it has eyes. Blinking eyes. Blinking. Blinking.

"What if she's not breathing?"

"Where's Mom and Dad?" he asks softly.

"Ottawa."

"Okay, stay calm, okay. You need to go back to wherever she is. That's your first step. Maybe she's okay. And, in the worst-case scenario, if she's not okay, you need to call the police and tell them to get an ambulance. Can you do that?"

"Okay." Suddenly, I just start sobbing again, shoulders shaking, hiccupping. I need air. Air to my lungs. *"Brad . . . what . . . have . . . I . . . done?"*

"Nova, breathe. Slow down for a sec. And listen to me. You must act here, and fast. I wish I weren't so far away but I am. So what you need to do is hang up, get it together and go back to where you left her and, if need be, call for an ambulance."

I wipe my face. "I just left her. That's what I did. I left her with blood all over her. How could I be so awful?"

"Forget that. Go, Nova. Now."

"I need to call Izzy. She'll come and help me."

"That's a good idea," says Brad. "But please, please, just get back to wherever you left her. I'm going to hang up. And you, GO."

I run down the hall and press the elevator button, once, twice. "Come on! Come on!" I cry. "Come on!"

Again. Again.

Finally, I hear it. I hear it rumbling. "Come on, come on, come on."

The doors open and it's empty. Thank god. I press Lobby. As it moves, I put my hands against the wall to hold me up. I want to buckle, fall, lie on the ground. I feel dizzy, disoriented. I inhale and exhale, inhale and exhale. My hands flutter as I keep making myself breathe. The elevator sinks to the bottom, and when the doors open I rush outside and into the fresh air, but it makes me feel nothing, not hot or cold, or anything, but numb. That's it. My body feels numb, as if I'm floating outside of it. My legs automatically kick into gear and I start to run back to where I left her. I have to call Izzy. I have to call Izzy. Oh god, what have I done?

"Nova?" says Izzy, obviously half asleep.

"I need you to come." My words rush out of me. "I've done something awful."

"It's three thirty in the morning," says Izzy. "Where are you?"

"Please. Please." I start crying again, tears that won't stop. "I think I'm a murderer."

CHAPTER 9
LAST NOVEMBER

School intensifies. The homework piles up and I spend a lot of time in my room doing assignments and labs. Weeks go by in a blur of essays, midterms and trying to find time to be with a boyfriend who swims for two teams. I offer to tutor him just so we can spend time together. I want to mention the brush, but I don't. Every time I try, a lump appears in my throat. Anyway, I followed him and Jada once in the halls and he didn't even touch her. That convinced me that they had nothing going on.

"I've missed you," I say to Leo. I lean into him, just to feel his body. We're hanging out in the library during the one spare we have together during the week. "It's already mid-November. Thanksgiving and Halloween seem like ages ago."

He shrugs. "It's the way it is."

"I know."

He touches my hair. "I'm so pumped for this weekend. We're going to kick butt."

I move away from him. That isn't what I wanted him to say. Doesn't he miss me too? Since my birthday weekend, we've probably had a handful of real dates, and we usually end up in his bed. He was gone away one weekend for a club meet, and the other weekends he had intense training. I get it. All he needs to do is tell me that he misses me too. Since we had sex, it seems to me as if things have changed. I get that life has ramped up. He's swimming on two teams and trying to keep up at school, and I'm studying like crazy, trying to win the academic award.

He drops his hand. "What's wrong?"

"Nothing," I retort.

"Could have fooled me." He sits back and taps his pencil on his notebook.

"It's just that we've hardly seen each other lately. Sure, we hang out at school, but we don't have dates anymore." I pause. "And I seriously miss you."

"Nova, swimming is my priority. I need fast times for next year."

Next year seems a long way away, but then it doesn't. I put in my application for the University of Toronto already. Since I'm staying in Toronto — no choice there — I'll be close to Michigan, where Leo is going. It's only a five-hour drive. I could get there for a long weekend. Catch a bus or something. I want us to stay together after high school. We're meant to grow old together.

"I don't want to think about next year yet," I say. I put my hand on his thigh.

"I do," he says. "It's all I can think about." He sits up, and our shoulders aren't connected anymore, and my hand gets moved. He turns to face me. "Did I tell you I talked to the coach the other day?"

Excitement exudes from his face, and I know that it has nothing to do with me. Nothing.

"That's great," I say, trying to be enthusiastic.

I listen as he gives me a blow-by-blow of the conversation. How they want him there in early August. How he will go to Michigan in the spring for yet another tour. How he can't wait to be on campus, go to football games, train in a huge pool. He sounds so excited. Where do I fit?

Do I even fit?

I have to fit.

His voice is so full of energy. But then he takes a break from talking and puts his arm around me. His touch sends warm shivers through my entire body, and it makes me feel like we will be okay. Every part of my body wants him, needs him. We still have months until he leaves. Why am I thinking so far ahead when it's not even Christmas yet?

I lean into him and try to absorb some of his energy. Plus I want to be close to him.

"Are you coming to watch the meet on the weekend?" he asks.

"Yeah, for sure," I say. He's never once asked me if I miss swimming or even said he misses me being on the team.

"I bet Jada wins overall for the females."

My back straightens. Why did he have to bring her up? A vision of her brushing her hair flashes in my mind. That pink, shiny brush. I'm stinging so much inside that he mentioned her now, when we were having a conversation about *us*, that I just blurt out, "Why was Jada's brush in your room?"

Leo frowns at me. "What are you talking about?"

"I, uh, saw her brush in your room."

"When?"

"After my birthday?"

He bursts out laughing. "That was over a month ago. Why are you bringing it up now?"

"You never answered me. Why was it in your room?"

Still laughing, he says, "Nova, come on now. It fell out of her bag when we were carpooling. My mother thought it was yours." He nuzzles his nose into my hair. "Your brush would have smelled so much better than hers."

I exhale a huge sigh of relief, and lean back into him. My body tingles with his touch and I feel as if I could be swallowed up inside of him. Why did I doubt him?

Once again, I put my hand on his thigh. He reaches down, looks around, then he moves it up so it's on the fly of his jeans. Then he whispers, "I have missed you, Nova. Big-time. Why don't we ditch this place and go find someplace private?"

"You mean to do . . . what I think you mean?"

He puts his arm around me and whispers softly in my ear, "Oh, yeah."

"Um, I'm not sure about that." And I'm not. When I'm at school, I work. And anyway, where would we go? To his car?

Then I see Jada pushing open the door to the library. She gives Leo a huge wave and flashes him a smile. Today she's in skin-tight jeans and an even tighter T-shirt.

"Okay," I whisper. "You lead."

We need to walk by Jada to get out of the library, and when Leo stops to talk to her, I give him a little shove on the back. "No time," I whisper. I can't believe I'm going to do this.

He smiles back at me and winks. Jada looks confused, but I keep my hand on Leo's back.

I make sure I'm giggling loudly when he pushes the door open and we walk into the hallway. Leo leads. I follow. To a back corner of the school that I didn't even know existed.

CHAPTER 10
POOL PALS

What I don't tell Leo before the swim meet is that I'm nervous about how I'll feel watching my former teammates race. I quit. Gave up. I'm so relieved I did, but this first meet might be a killer. But to whine about my feelings before he swims would be mean. So I say nothing.

"Please, come with me," I beg Izzy. We are walking out of the school on Friday afternoon.

"Yeah, sure," she says. "Felix said he wants to go too. Experience the rah-rah of Canadian sports. I told him to watch a hockey game, not a swim meet, but whatever. We'll go to the swim meet."

"Great," I say. "I have Leo's times."

Izzy tilts her head and stares at me. "You guys okay?"

"Yeah. We're okay. Why do you ask?"

"I don't know. You're not PDA-ing all over the school. What's going on?"

I shrug. *We did it in a back hallway so maybe we don't need to PDA.* We walk a few strides before I ask, "Do you think about you and Felix next year?"

Izzy tosses her head and her dark hair swings under her beret. "Yes and no. I'm trying to live in the moment and enjoy life right now."

"I'm not so good at that." I pause. "Since we had sex, it just seems like things are off." Again, the tears lurk behind my eyes. I'm like a walking fountain. "It's like that's the only thing he wants. He won't talk about our future. It's like I won't exist after graduation. I see us together forever."

"Hey." She slings her arm around me. "This is a tough year for everyone. We all have these huge choices to make. And we're all moving on."

"I don't know what's wrong with me. I've never thought of myself as a clingy person. But the thought of not being with him next year is something I can't seem to handle."

She squeezes my shoulder. "Hormones, girl, hormones. They'll get you every time."

I laugh as I discreetly wipe my face. "That's it." I nudge her with my shoulder. "I looked up online about why my period is so screwy and found out that quitting a sport cold turkey like I quit swimming could cause that to happen. So, yeah, hormones."

She bumps me back. "You sound like a doctor. You do know you're the one who will be the doctor tomorrow. And Leo will have nothing to do with that. When he's old with a paunch belly and no longer swimming, you're going to be the one who's on top."

"Thanks," I say. "I needed that today." And I did too. I can picture us together like that, later in our lives.

"Senior year is about living in the moment," Izzy says. "And in this moment, I want a coffee. Pit stop?"

"For sure." I link my arm in hers.

* * *

I enter the pool area on Saturday and smell the chlorine. I inhale. Do I miss this? Suddenly, it hits me that I don't. Not even a little bit. Here I was worried about how I was going to feel about this meet and . . . I feel nothing. Not even a little regret, except that when I swam, I got to see Leo more.

I sit down by myself, saving two spots for Izzy and Felix. They walk in just as Leo takes to the pool deck, wearing his bathing cap and goggles. When I see Izzy scanning the crowd, looking for me, I wave. They join me just as Leo gets on the starter block. I clasp my hands together as I stare at his perfect body. Long limbs, muscles, zero fat. The guy is built like a god, and he picked me to be his girlfriend.

The gun goes off and Leo does a perfect dive into the pool. He surfaces and starts his smooth and rhythmical strokes. Within seconds he's ahead. He turns at the wall and resurfaces. I think of Jada going on and on about how they worked together on turns to cut their time. I shake my head. She's not the one who made out with him in the hidden-from-everyone school hallway.

Leo wins his freestyle heat by half a length of the pool. Seriously. Half a length. No one even comes close to him. The crowd cheers; lots of students have shown up for the meet.

"Does the guy have flippers for feet?" Felix laughs.

"More or less," I answer. "And the wingspan of a bird. When I was swimming, I had neither of those."

Felix looks around at the many students waving school flags, wearing school colours. "He has a fan club."

"That he does," I say. I look back at the pool and see Leo taking off his cap and goggles. His next race is another hour away. He'll head to the hot tub for a bit.

"You guys hungry? Leo isn't up for a bit. We should have time before his backstroke event."

"I could eat," says Izzy.

Felix grins. "You can always eat. And you never put on an ounce."

"Oh, you, be quiet." Izzy makes a cute face at Felix. Then she kisses his cheek.

We get up and, as we're walking down the bleacher stairs, I see Leo talking to Jada. She's wearing her cap and her goggles are perched on her forehead. She's up soon for her breaststroke heat. Jada gives Leo a hug, and to me it seems to linger. I think about how only a Lycra bathing suit is between their skin. Izzy prods my back. "Keep walking," she says. Then she leans into me and whispers, "And quit torturing yourself."

"She's after him," I whisper. "I know it and you know it."

"Hmmmmm." Izzy stares over at them. Then she turns to me and says, "Maybe. Maybe not, though. They could just be good friends because of common interests." She whispers in my ear. "I think he's into you, my friend. Let's get some food."

Izzy and I both order salads, and Felix gets a hamburger. For breakfast, I had coffee and a smoothie, so I'm starving, or I think I am. Once I start eating, though, the food just sits in my stomach. It seems to plunge down and land with a thud. I need to stop worrying about Leo and Jada. I push everything around my plate, and when Felix offers me one of his french fries, I eat it. It tastes a whole lot better than the salad. Like comfort food. Maybe that's what I need.

"I'm going to get fries too," I say.

I share them with Izzy, but I eat well over half. Each one tastes better than the last. For some reason they ease my insecurities.

We head back to the pool area, going by the community centre gym. Treadmills, ellipticals and bikes all surround the track area. And inside the track are all the weight machines. I stop for a second and stare. I don't miss swimming, but I do miss being physical. I don't want my body to turn to mush. I turn to Izzy.

"We should come work out sometime."

Izzy laughs. "Sure. Why not? I love getting sweaty and hot."

"No, I'm serious. We should come here for workouts. Better than the school gym. This gym has everything and is close. We could come a few times a week."

"I was looking for a gym," says Felix.

"We could all go," I say.

Izzy shrugs. "Okay," she says. "I'm game. Why not? I can pedal a bike."

We sit back down to watch the rest of the races. Race after race goes by. Leo is in every event. Jada and Leo win all their heats. Every single one.

Then the heats for female freestyle relay team get announced.

I pull out my phone and pretend to look at my text messages. My mom has sent one, wondering if I'm going to be home for dinner. Since the meet is two days long, I know I won't be seeing Leo tonight. He never parties while competing.

I turn to Izzy and Felix to ask what they are doing later, and I see their hands intertwined. Izzy has this look of contentment on her face. Something I've never seen with her. I don't want to be the odd man out, so I turn back to the pool, in time to see our school win the female relay race.

I text my mother back.

Home for dinner.

At the end of the meet, I walk out with Felix and Izzy.

"You seeing Leo later?" Izzy asks.

"No," I answer. "He'll have to rest up for tomorrow."

"We were just going to wander around downtown. Explore a bit. Felix has never been to the top of the CN Tower." She grins at him.

"I hate heights," says Felix.

She laughs. "Don't be such a wuss. Join us, Nova."

"Nah," I say. "It's okay. I got homework to do."

"It's Saturday," says Felix. "No one should do homework on a Saturday. That's a British rule. Saturdays are for fish and chips. No wait. That's Friday." He laughs.

"What about tea?" I ask. "High tea." I pretend to do a British accent.

He sticks his nose in the air and says, "Oh blimey, I forgot about tea." As he pretends to talk like the queen, I laugh, because Felix does have a wicked sense of humour.

"CN Tower, here we come," says Izzy. "And no tea."

"You guys go." I give them both a gentle little push. "I'm not into the CN Tower either, Felix. The glass floor makes me sick."

"Let's go to the beach then," says Izzy. "I can shift plans in a heartbeat."

"I'm good, you guys." I wave my hands at them. "I think my dad's home tonight anyway. I can watch a movie with him."

"Your call," says Izzy. "Text later if your parents are driving you crazy."

"Will do."

We split up at the subway station. And I watch them get on their train. They're so cute together, and I'm honestly happy for Izzy. She's had so many boyfriends, none of whom she's acted like this with. They wave as the train moves. I wave back and take in a big breath of air. Then I exhale, wanting everything stale out of my body. Leo and I used to be like them, all cuddly and doing things on a Saturday night. I need to get us back to that. Maybe quitting the swim team wasn't my best move. We'd be together tonight, maybe going out for a quick bite to eat. Is he out with the team right now, sitting beside Jada?

I shake my head. I can't do this to myself. But as I get on the subway, the thoughts of them being together don't leave my mind, and they make my stomach sick. The fries are sitting heavy in the pit of it, rolling around. I find a seat, but the lurching of the train doesn't help make my stomach feel any better. Is he with Jada? Are they cozied up together somewhere? Is she rubbing her shoulder up against his?

I blow out air and put my hand on my stomach to make it stop flip-flopping. I can't let her do this to me.

CHAPTER 11
DAD ON THE DECK

I arrive home and my mother has made a shepherd's pie for dinner. I don't really feel like eating but I help set the table. I only see two placemats, so I get two plates.

"Looks good," I say to be nice. Lately, she hasn't had time to cook, so this is kind of a big deal. "Where's Dad?"

"He's going to be a bit late. But he'll be home around eight."

"We could wait," I say.

"It's okay. He said to go ahead."

We sit down, and she starts dishing out the meal. "What are your plans for tonight?"

"I've got some homework."

"How was the swim meet?" She hands me my plate.

I shrug. "I don't really want to talk about it." Suddenly, I'm exhausted. It's like a heavy blanket has descended on me, and every muscle and bone in my body is tired. I try to hide a yawn from my mother. I'm not sure why I'm tired when I didn't exert any energy today.

"I'm sure it's hard to watch," says my mother. "Do you think you did the right thing by quitting?"

"I think so," I say.

"Maybe you should try running."

The thought of running in this moment makes me want to throw up again. I could curl up right here at the table and fall asleep. "I, uh, saw the gym equipment at the community centre. I might start working out there. They have a great rate for students."

"Running doesn't cost a thing," she says.

"I think I know that."

Thankfully, she stops talking to eat a mouthful of food. We both eat in silence for a few minutes. Then she asks, "How did Leo do?"

"He won all his heats by at least half a length. No one is even close to him."

"I wonder if we'll see him at the Olympics one day. That takes such dedication and time. I can't help but notice he's not around very often."

I push my green peas and hamburger around the plate. Is she trying to tell me something? Being subtle has never been her strength.

"You okay?" She asks. "Is everything okay with you and Leo?"

Yeah, we had sex. Is that what you want to know? We had sex and now I think he likes someone else, and it makes me feel sick and tired.

"I'm just tired, Mom."

"It's probably because you aren't exercising. Your body might be going through withdrawals. You did stop cold turkey."

"Ohmygod. You make it sound like I was on drugs. I was swimming!"

"That's not what I meant. Maybe I used the wrong word. But you exercised every day and now you're not doing anything. That's hard on the body."

"Okay, okay. I quit. I get it. I'm a quitter. Is that what you want me to say?"

"It's not what I'm saying at all, Nova."

I don't answer. I don't have the energy for her and her comments about my life. I get up and take my plate to the sink. After the dinner dishes are done, I go to my room and shut the door. I lie on my bed and close my eyes.

My body is exhausted.

When I wake up, it is eleven thirty. I don't hear the television or any voices. Did I sleep through my father coming home? I promised him we'd watch a movie together. I crawl out of bed and head out to the kitchen. The lights are all off, so I tread quietly. As I'm running the tap to get a drink of water, I see my dad through the glass balcony doors, the outline of his body. He's sitting on a chair, outside on our small apartment deck, by himself.

Water in hand, I slide open the door and peer out. City lights shine.

"Hey, Dad," I say quietly.

"Hey, kiddo. How are you?"

I step onto the deck, glad I'm wearing a hoodie, as there is definitely a winter feel to the air. I sit down on the other deck chair. The balcony only fits two chairs and a little bistro table, plus a barbecue. He sips his whisky.

"I'm okay. Sorry I fell asleep. Did you and Mom watch a movie?"

"Yeah. No worries. I checked on you and you were sound asleep."

"School is tough this year," I say.

"You miss swimming?"

"Not really. It's kind of weird. I liked it, but then I stopped liking it. If that makes sense. I went to the meet today and didn't feel the urge to jump in a pool. And I want good marks. I don't think I can do both."

"Good for you. You've got your head on straight."

Since I don't want to talk about me, and I have a feeling that comment was more about Brad than me, I ask, "How are you?"

"Oh, I've been better." He gives a funny little laugh. Then he twirls his glass, the ice tinkling against the side. "But I'll get something here soon."

"You will, Dad." Then I just say, "I'm so sorry things are still so hard."

"Not your fault."

"I'm sure you'll get another job." I sip my water. Lately he's had two final interviews, only to lose out in the end.

He lets go a huge sigh. "I should go join Brad on the beach."

I laugh at this. "Yeah, maybe he's got it figured out more than we do."

"Do you talk to him, ever?"

I want to lie, but we don't have too many heart-to-heart conversations, so I say, "Sometimes. We text quite a bit." I look out to the night sky. It's cloudy and dark, no stars. But the city lights shine through the low light. This is the only thing that I like about the apartment, is being on the deck at night and seeing the city.

"Next time you talk, tell him I miss him." Then he downs his drink.

"I will," I say. "I miss him too."

He sighs and stands. "I'm going to bed."

"Me too," I say.

I head back to my room, crawl under the covers, and sleep until morning.

CHAPTER 12
IN LOVE

School doesn't slow down, so Izzy and I don't get to the gym until the weekend. Leo is out of town at a swim meet with his club team. Of course, Jada-flipper-feet is on that team too. Argh. It makes me crazy thinking of them together. A workout will do me good.

"So give me the goods, here," says Izzy. "What should I do?"

She is wearing grey sweatpants that are too big for her and some Rolling Stones T-shirt that I'm sure is her father's. At least she has her hair pulled back in a headband.

"Nice outfit," I say.

"Next time lend me some *Lycra*." She mocks the word *Lycra* and I laugh. I'm dressed in Lycra tights and a tank top.

Felix shakes his head at Izzy, laughing. "You're something else," he says to her.

Izzy shrugs. "Gotta be an individual in this world."

"Oh, you're that all right," he says, with this affection that is so intimate.

"I'm going to run on the treadmill for thirty, then do weights," I say. "I made up a little workout on my phone."

"Weights?" Izzy flexes her bicep. "I'll join you for that action."

We get on the treadmills, and Felix and I run while Izzy walks. With a good playlist going through my earbuds, the thirty minutes zips by. I towel off and inhale. Then I exhale. I needed this so badly. Izzy joins me in doing the weight workout I set up, and Felix goes off to do his own thing.

Izzy watches him walk away. Then she turns to me with a smirk. "This was a great idea. I like seeing him in a muscle shirt."

I throw my towel at her. "Focus," I say. Then I pick up two ten-pound weights and give them to her. I take the twenties. "First exercise is bicep curl. Ten reps."

The workout lasts forty-five minutes, and by the time we're done I'm drenched in sweat. So is Izzy.

"I hate to admit," she said. "But that felt good. I'm going to hurt tomorrow, though."

"Me too," I said. "Let's find Felix."

Felix tells us he needs another thirty minutes to finish his workout, so we tell him to meet us in the cafeteria. We shower, dry our hair and head to the cafeteria. After filling up our water bottles, we find a table that isn't covered in ketchup packets. And one away from the mother who has four screaming kids.

I plunk down on a hard, plastic chair. "Thanks for joining me."

"You're a slave driver. You know that, right?" Izzy sits down and makes a face. "My ass is gonna be mad tomorrow."

I laugh and sip my water. "It's good for you. And something you can do with Felix since he's into it too."

"Oh, believe me, I have more than enough to do with Felix."

"So . . ."

She squeals, and when the screaming kids all look her way, she claps her hand over her mouth. "Little ears don't need to hear this, but . . ."

"But . . . what?"

She sucks on air, closes her eyes, breathes out, then opens her eyes wide. She leans closer to me and whispers, "It was spectacular. Like outta this world."

"Spectacular? Wow. That's a new word." I try to be happy, because I am happy for her, but my body sags. Leo and I rushed sex in a back hallway where I tried to have a good time, but the thought of getting caught never left me the entire time. What if he figured it out and wants someone who can just do it anywhere?

Izzy reaches across and puts her hand on mine. "This isn't my first guy. I've had a few duds."

"Spare me the details."

"Maybe you're not relaxed. I mean you are kind of an intense human. It's what I love about you, but try to Zen a little more."

"Zen? Okay. Sure. That might make me fall asleep."

"Okay, don't do that."

I sigh. "I just love Leo so much that I want it to be . . . spectacular."

She leans back in her chair and eyes me, her head tilted to the side. "You. Love. Him?" She asks slowly, her words spaced out. "I've never heard you say that before."

"I wouldn't miss him if I didn't love him. When he's away, my heart aches for him. That's love, Izzy."

She shrugs. "Maybe. But you might also just be a bit bored with not swimming anymore and have more time and he doesn't. So you think you're in love."

"I had sex with him. I've always wanted to wait to do it with the love of my life. I want to have a life with him after high school too."

"Yeah, okay. You always did say you were waiting for the love part first." She looks at me. "But . . . has he ever told you he loves you?"

"No."

"Have you told him?"

"No." I need to change the topic. "You and Felix are into each other big-time."

"We have a good time together. With him it's a love for fun and experiences."

I think about the words *fun* and *experience*. When was the last time Leo and I had fun? At my birthday dinner. Maybe Izzy is right, I do need to relax. Let go of Jada. Maybe I should plan something fun for us to do.

I see Izzy looking over my shoulder and I turn and see Felix walking toward us. He is looking at her like she looks at him, all googly-eyed.

"I'm starving," he says, when he approaches the table. "Did you eat?"

"Nope," I say. "We're waiting for you."

He punches his chest in a Tarzan-like move. "That felt a-maz-ing. Thanks, Nova!" His accent makes the word amazing sound . . . well, amazing. Izzy and I both laugh at him.

At the concession stand, I order a sandwich and fries. Izzy gets the same. She playfully shoulders me. "This kind of defeats the workout."

"Who cares," I say.

"I'm with ya," she replies. Then she holds up her hand for a high-five.

Back at the table, I suddenly realize I'm absolutely starving. The tomato in the sandwich looks gross and almost makes me want to barf. I wrap it in a paper serviette. Then I eat everything on my plate.

Maybe having a plan is exactly what me and Leo need. I'm excited to plan something that will pull us closer.

I need to show him just how much I do love him.

CHAPTER 13
THE PLAN

The magical Christmas Market becomes my plan. Every year the Distillery District brings Christmas cheer to the city of Toronto. Colourful Christmas lights are strung on storefronts. Most of the shops have gone all out with their Christmas displays. Wreaths hangs on doors, garland loops from window to window and different variations of Santa and his reindeers, angels and old-fashioned winter scenes are cleverly positioned in windows. Everything twinkles. All day and night live music takes to a stage, and the sound of different groups and choirs singing Christmas music fills the air.

I pull on Leo's arm. "Let's stop and listen."

We move closer to the crowd of people surrounding the carolers on stage. They sing in perfect harmony, "Little Drummer Boy." My favourite Christmas song. There is such a festive feeling. But more so this year because I'm sharing it with Leo. I lean my head against him, and it feels so good to have him close to me. We stand there for a few minutes, listening to the song. A warmth radiates through me. The song ends.

He turns to me. "Let's get something to eat."

"Okay," I say.

"Not here, though. Everything is so expensive."

He's right about that, but I kind of wanted to stay at the market a little longer. Enjoy the festivities. It doesn't cost anything to walk around, but when he's hungry, he's hungry.

"Let's get a photo before we go." I make him stand by a tree decorated in twinkly white lights and white angels. I snap a selfie of us. Something to post on social media.

He wants a cheap pizza, so we catch the King streetcar over to Yonge Street. The entire time we're sitting on the streetcar he's checking his phone. I have no idea who he's texting because he doesn't talk to me. So I look at my phone and post the photo. By the time we get off the streetcar, I have lots of likes, heart emojis and comments about how sweet we look together. I smile. It's a great shot of both of us.

Off the streetcar, we trudge through some light snow to his favourite pizza place. Cost is ten dollars for a large. As soon as the calendar switched to December, winter arrived. It's cold, but not freezing, the wind off the lake not too drastic. I'm still bundled up anyway, wearing a trendy scarf. We order the large pizza, but I tell myself that I can only eat one piece. After doing some research online, I discovered that the pill can cause weight gain. I've noticed my jeans are getting a big snug. Not what I want. Not before Christmas.

"I'm loving my workouts at the gym," I say to make conversation. I take a bite of the hot pizza.

"What kind of workouts?" He keeps his head down, engrossed in his food.

"I've adapted some of the swimming weight workouts we used to do and just added some other stuff."

"We aren't lifting a whole lot right now."

"You guys are killing it, though." Our school is number one in the city.

"Yeah, it's been great," he says. "We're strong this year. We'll win the title for sure." He takes another piece of pizza.

I still feel a twinge when we talk about the high school team. "How's your club team?"

"Good. But, man, workouts are hard." He looks at his phone. "I've got to get home, like, ASAP. I have an early-morning club swim."

"Sure," I say.

We finish the pizza, and I ate more than I wanted to. When we head back outside, I link my arm in his. "That was fun," I say.

"It was okay," he replies.

"What? I thought it was fun."

He stops and pulls me toward him. Then he kisses me right there on the street. When we break apart, he says, "My parents are gone again in a couple of weeks. You should sleep over again. Now that's my idea of fun."

"Sure," I say. I look to the ground. So much for my plans.

* * *

It's only ten when I get home. I walk into the living room, and my mother is sitting in her chair, lamp on, reading a book. She looks up at me.

"You're home early."

"Leo has morning practice."

"Sit with me for a few minutes," she says.

I point to her book. "I, uh, don't want to interrupt." I glance around. "Where's Dad?" I ask.

She gives me a funny look and a little shrug. "He's on the deck. Having his drink." She turns from me, and I think it's so I can't see her face.

"It's probably getting cold out there," I say.

"You want a cup of tea?" she asks.

Since it's early and I have nothing else to do on a Friday night, I say, "Sure."

Mom makes us tea and we sit in the living room. She puts her book away. I drink my tea and think about how to say what I want to say. I have something to tell her.

Finally, I say, "I talked to Brad today." My brother texted me and told me about the elephant sanctuary he'd been to in Thailand. It sounded fascinating. I want to tell Mom to make her think better of him, bridge the gap a little.

"Oh," she says. She puts her hands together. "By text?" she asks.

I nod. I know he doesn't talk to Mom or Dad.

"He's doing fine, Mom. Today he was at an elephant sanctuary, feeding these elephants who've had a tough go of it."

"He won't return my texts," she says. "He needs to come home for Christmas."

I glance around our apartment. Our house is gone. Now we have this little tree in the corner, and all our old decorations look as if they are crammed everywhere. We don't have a fireplace, so the stockings aren't up. It's so depressing.

"Where would he sleep?" I ask.

"I can clean up the spare bedroom."

Right now, the spare bedroom — which is smaller than mine and more like this tiny office — is crammed full of junk and boxes. "It's a mess," I say.

"If I knew he was coming, I'd get it done, Nova."

"Yeah, but he's not coming."

She shakes her head. "What have we done to him?"

"Mom, he was helping elephants. That's doing something good."

She sighs, smiles at me and gives this weird head nod. Her eyes look glassy. Is she crying about Brad? "He was always compassionate toward animals."

Since I know she's trying really hard not to break down, I change the subject. "I got ninety-nine per cent on my bio midterm."

"Nova, that's wonderful." She puts her hand on mine. "Remember education —"

"— is important." I cut her off mid-sentence. "Mom, you've told me that a million times. And, believe me, I get it. And don't worry. I love school. I won't quit."

CHAPTER 14
GOOD NEWS IS NO NEWS

At school on Monday morning, my Biology teacher, Mrs. Yildiz, asks me to stay after class. Students saunter out and I walk up to the front by her desk.

"Nova," she says. "I was wondering if you wanted some extra students to tutor. I know you tutor in math, but I have quite a few students in grade nine and ten science who could use some extra help."

"Sure," I say. "Extra money for university is always a good thing."

"That's terrific news," she smiles. "I've heard good things about your tutoring. A lot of parents and teachers are really happy with the job you're doing."

"Thanks," I say. "I appreciate you telling me."

"Keep at it. You really do have a strong future in science."

I'm smiling from ear to ear when I leave the classroom. I text Leo. *Where are u?*

I want to tell him my good news in person. When I don't get an answer, I know I need to get to my next class. My news will have to wait until lunch.

At lunch I race to the cafeteria. When I get there, I see him already at the lunch table, sitting beside Jada. My body goes ice-cold. I shake my head. They swim together and nothing else, or that's what I keep telling myself. I head over to the table and Leo is so engrossed in looking at Jada's phone that he doesn't hear me come up behind him. They have their heads bowed to the phone reading something. I wrap my arms around his neck.

He turns to me. "Nova," he says. "Where'd you come from?"

Jada moves over and I squeeze in between them.

"What were you guys looking at?" I ask.

"Canadian swim team time trials. What we need to get to make it," says Leo.

"You're close," says Jada. She holds up her crossed fingers. "This close."

"So are you." He puts his fingers in a circle as if to give her the a-okay.

Jada is going out for National Team too? This makes me sink inside.

"Wow," I say. "That's great, Leo." I knew that he was in conversations with Canada's National Team coach, and he did try out for the team last summer and was one of the last ones cut. But now Jada too. Suddenly, my news about tutoring kids who aren't doing well in science sounds a bit lame. I open my lunch and see the salad I packed. Forget that.

"Anyone want anything?" I stand up to head to the kitchen area of the cafeteria.

"Yeah, I'll take a chocolate milk if you're going," says Leo. He reaches in his pockets for money.

"No worries," I say. "I got it."

I head toward the cafeteria area. When I see that poutine is one of the daily specials, I put in my order.

* * *

After school, Izzy and I head to the gym. Felix is busy so we're on our own. Lately, I've only seen Izzy when she's with Felix. With Leo gone so much, I'm often that odd man out. Neither of them mind, but still, I'd like to have Leo with me sometimes. I get undressed and into my gym clothes. That's when I notice I've started my period. Weird. The pill has definitely not made me regular.

"Not again," I say. I dig in my gym bag.

"What's up?" Izzy asks.

"My period has come out of the blue. I just had it two weeks ago and it was so light, it lasted like one day. Now, it looks like it's doing the same thing."

"Lucky you. Wish mine were just spots instead of gushing fountains." She reaches in her bag. "I've got something."

Five minutes later, we head down to the gym area with our water bottles. As we go around a corner, I see the huge Christmas tree. Big green and red balls dangle from the fake branches. "What are you getting Felix for Christmas?" I ask.

Izzy takes a big swig from her water bottle. "We talked about it and decided that we'll give each other an experience."

"Oh, that's cool. So what are you giving him?"

"I asked my mom if I could borrow her car and she said yes, so we're going to hike the escarpment where all the waterfalls are. In Burlington."

"Ambitious."

She glances at me, grins and flexes her biceps. "I'm fit now."

I flex mine back and she grabs it. "Holy mackerel. You got real biceps happening."

"Only to get bigger when I up my weights."

We enter the gym. "So before I go torture myself with this workout nonsense, what are you getting Leo?" Izzy asks.

"I dunno. Maybe we should do the experience thing too. That

might be fun. Something different."

Izzy and I finish our workout and head to the cafeteria for a hot chocolate. We've just sat down when she looks at her phone and says, "Uh, oh. Have you seen this?"

"What?"

She hands me her phone. I look at the photo. My stomach sours. Jada is sitting on Leo's knee and she has her arm around his neck. I read the caption:

Swim team buds.

"Why does she have to post this crap?" My heart races just looking at how she's looking at him. "She's always posting stuff about her and Leo," I say. "It's so sickening."

"Yeah," says Izzy, "but the other stuff is like, 'look at how great we are *at swimming.*'" Izzy shakes her head. "This is the first one like this. Where it's almost more than swimming. I hate girls that go for guys that are taken."

I zoom in on the photo because I want to see Leo up close. Without looking up, I say, "He's not touching her."

"Let me see." Izzy takes her phone back and looks at the photo again. "You're right. Good for Leo."

"I found her brush in his room," I say.

"What?" Izzy stares at me, wide-eyed. "Why didn't you tell me that?"

I shrug. "It was ages ago. I asked him about it, and he said she left it in his car. So I hoped it was nothing."

"In all fairness," says Izzy, "that could be true. Just the other day, I left my sunglasses in Felix's car. Didn't even know I'd done that."

Something inside of me doesn't feel right. It's as if I have rotting food in my stomach.

"I think I hate her right now," I say.

CHAPTER 15
EXPECTATIONS

"What should we watch?" I ask Leo.

He's at my place for a change. Two more days and it's Christmas break. We sit in my room, on the floor, leaning against my bed. My computer is open, and we're going to watch a Christmas movie. He tickles me. Then he nuzzles his nose into my neck.

"Why do we have to watch something?" He sticks his hand under my sweater.

I laugh and playfully punch him. "It's Christmas. We need to watch the Grinch."

He moans. "I've seen it a million times."

"That's the point. It's a movie you watch every Christmas."

He kisses my neck. "I've got a better idea." He speaks in this low, growly voice, which sounds like Jim Carrey in *How the Grinch Stole Christmas*, and it makes me laugh even harder.

"We can't tonight," I say.

"Why?"

"I don't know. Maybe because my mom is in the other room." The thought of doing it with my mother in the apartment makes me feel all anxious. What if she walked in on us? Or even knocked on my door when we were naked. To me, that is not an option. I wouldn't be able to relax, and I don't want to have bad sex with Leo.

"Can't we lock your door?" He continues kissing my neck.

It feels so good to have him kiss me. Warm air swirls around me, the tingles all still there. We've had such little time together, lately, but I gently push him away. "Not tonight," I whisper. "In case you haven't noticed, I now live in a box."

"Okay. Let's watch *Love Actually*. I'm sick of the Grinch."

I get the movie on and turn off the light. We sit back and watch. We don't talk. He doesn't even hold my hand. It's like he doesn't want to touch me if we aren't having sex. Halfway through, I pause the movie. "I'll make popcorn," I say.

"Sure."

Mom is in the kitchen, and she glances at me when I get out the hot air popper. "You can watch television in the living room too," she says.

"We're good," I say.

"I trust you," she says.

What is that supposed to mean? Well, I know what it means. Why does she have to say it, though? I'm seventeen years old. I refuse to make eye contact. The popcorn popping is a needed sound because it drowns out the silence. Without saying another word to my mother, I add butter and salt and take the popcorn back to my room. Leo is texting someone, his phone bright in the darkened room.

"Who you talking to?" I ask.

"Jada."

Something cools inside me. No. Freezes. But I try to act casual as I sit down beside him. "What's she up to?"

"Family Christmas party."

"Oh, that's nice." I never did mention the photo she posted to him, and it got taken down. She had so many negative comments about being a boyfriend stealer.

"Speaking of Christmas," I say. "I have an idea for our gifts."

"I haven't even thought of gifts yet," he says.

I nudge my shoulder against his, so we're touching. Then I kiss his neck. "We could do experiences," I say.

"Like kinky sex?"

"Nooooooo." I laugh, and playfully pat his chest. "Not that kind of experience. Like something fun that we could do together."

"Like what?" He takes a handful of popcorn and shoves it in his mouth.

"I don't know. Maybe an evening at a live play. Or a hike by the escarpment. Stuff like that."

He turns and stares at me. "Seriously, Nova. I barely have time to breathe with my schedule. The last thing I need is to be out hiking on a day off."

Something sinks inside of me. And it feels like a block of ice has hit my heart. I suck in air, but feel the damn tears lurking behind my eyes.

"Should we turn the movie back on?" he asks.

I nod.

We don't talk much for the rest of the movie. I try to laugh at the funny parts, but it's hard. I'm still stinging at his complete dismissal of my idea. Why am I being so emotional? By the end of the movie, I've successfully stopped the tears. Am I becoming the needy girlfriend? Could I be driving him away? The movie credits roll. The room is still dark. I lean my head against him.

"Should we watch another movie?" I ask.

He checks his phone. "I should get going," he says.

"Understand," I say. "Did you hear anything more about the National Team?" I want to keep him here, and I know that swimming is something he'll talk about.

"Tryouts are coming up." He puts his arm around me. "I'm going to make it this time."

"I know you will." I kiss his cheek.

"I know I'm on the right track." He talks as if he's giving himself a pep talk. "I can't wait to get to college too. Did I tell you I'm going for a visit in March?"

I snuggle closer to him. "You did tell me," I say.

"I'm just so ready for that life. It's going to be so exciting."

I think about that. He'll be away, and I'll be living at home and commuting by streetcar and subway.

"Since I'm definitely staying in Toronto, I can come visit you," I say. "It's only a five-hour drive."

Suddenly, his body stiffens. He pushes away from me.

"What?" I stare at him and can see the white of his eyes in the dark. "You don't want me to?"

"I don't know. Who knows what will happen between now and then."

"Oh," I say. I lower my head.

He lifts my chin. "I don't want us to break up yet. But long distance is tough. And I'm going to be all-consumed. College swimming is intense. And if I add National Team to that, then there goes even more time. I mean, I could be gone all summer long too."

I nod. "So I'm not in any of your plans?" I sound whiny. My voice cracks.

"We'll be going in different directions. Life after high school is different than life in high school. What do you expect from me?"

"I don't expect anything?" I turn away from him. But I do. I want us together in rocking chairs.

"You obviously do, or we wouldn't even be talking about this."

"It's fine," I say. None of this is what I want to hear. Do I not fit into his plans? At all? Like not even a little bit? Lots of people do long-distance relationships. Why can't we?

He checks his phone again. Then he stands. "I should go." He pulls me toward him and kisses me. I kiss him back, and it's like I'm devouring him. I can't get enough of him. I run my hands up and down his back. Why didn't I say yes to his advances tonight? It might have kept him here longer.

When he pulls back, he starts to laugh. "Wow. I'll take that as my Christmas gift." He touches my cheek. "My parents are going away over Christmas. Let's plan a night."

I nod but don't speak. Yes, that's what we should do. And . . . exactly what I need to do to keep him wanting me.

CHAPTER 16
CHRISTMAS HOLIDAYS

Christmas morning dawns and I get out of bed, but I don't rush to the tree to open gifts. It's like there's this heavy feeling in our apartment. Brad isn't here. Brad and I always raced to the tree, laughing and pushing each other to be the one who got there first. Then we both sat down on the floor and unwrapped all our stocking gifts. Last Christmas, as old as we were, we'd slept in the same room on Christmas Eve. He'd come home from university for the break. Little did Mom and Dad know that even at that time he was struggling with his classes, skipping and hanging out, doing nothing. It wasn't long into the new year when he phoned and told my parents he'd quit university and was on a beach.

"Merry Christmas," I say to my mom and dad. First time ever they've been up before me.

"Merry Christmas, honey."

We sit around and do the gift opening, although the presents are minimal. I'm okay with that. I'm not a child and I understand money problems. We do our usual omelette breakfast, which is something that Brad always helped Dad with. It was our boys-make-breakfast tradition.

After breakfast, I go to my room and phone Leo.

"Merry Christmas," I say. I try to create joy in my voice.

"Back at ya," he replies. Then he says with real excitement in his voice, "You're not going to believe what my parents got me and my bro?"

"What?"

"A trip to an all-inclusive beach place in Cancún. We're ditching turkey dinner and leaving tonight. It's perfect. Mom even got me the week off from swimming. It's exactly the break I need before I'm back at swimming full-time. I'm packing right now."

"Oh, that's so fantastic." I try so hard to be thrilled for him, but the day is just not that exciting for me, and now he's going to be gone all week. He'll be hanging out on a beach, looking at girls in bikinis. "I'll miss you, though."

"I'm only gone ten days."

By his breathy voice I know he's throwing shorts and T-shirts into a suitcase.

"I know," I say, "but . . . I thought we could get together when your parents were gone." I try to use a seductive sort of voice. "Are you gone for New Year's?"

"Oh yeah, big party on the beach," he says.

I hear someone calling him, so I say, "Have a good trip. I'd better let you go."

* * *

All day my mother tries to be chipper, happy, and do all of our Christmas traditions, but it's pretty obvious that she's upset that my brother didn't come home. All of her efforts come off as fake. And my dad is super quiet. Just before we are to head to my grandparents', dressed in our Christmas clothes, we try to call Brad, but he doesn't answer.

When we get home later that night, I'm in turkey overload so I go to my bedroom. I glance at my phone and see Brad tried to call me by an audio call. I call him back.

"Hey, Nova. Merry Christmas to you!" He sounds upbeat too, in that Christmas way. I wonder if he's drunk or high.

"How's Christmas over there?" I ask.

"Weird. Different. But okay. Can't beat the heat."

"Mom and Dad really miss you."

There is silence on the other end of the phone. I hear him breathing. I wait. Then he says softly, "Not now, Nova. Not today. It's Christmas."

"That's my point. It's Christmas and you're not here."

"You don't understand. And don't worry, I'm going to make things right. But . . . they got to give a bit. Just an FYI, I'm doing this for you too. They need to stop pressuring us. I mean, Mom just puts all her mistakes on to us, and wants us to correct them through our actions. It's like we're not allowed to make any of our own."

"Yeah, I get that. She's on me all the time." I pause. "I quit swimming."

"Oh, I bet she wasn't happy about that."

"She's been okay with it. But thinks I'm going to have too much time to party."

"You still got the boyfriend?"

"Yeah. We're together."

"Don't have sex. She'll be on you about that one too. I got the talk every other week about not getting a girl pregnant. She was convinced I was going to ruin my life before I got to university."

There are things I can talk about with Brad, my brother, but sex isn't one of them. "You helped any more elephants?" I ask instead.

He laughs and tells me about Thailand. I lie on my bed, wishing I was there with him. Izzy is gone skiing with her family, and Leo is on a plane to Cancún. I'm stuck at home, in a small apartment, with my parents' lingering sadness about a brother who is languishing on a beach in Thailand.

When it's time to end our conversation, I say, "Phone Mom and Dad. I really think they might be trying to come around, and actually feel bad for putting pressure on you."

"I will," he says. "When the time is right."

* * *

Exams are in late January, so I spend my Christmas week in my room studying. I also sleep a lot. Or just stare at the ceiling. Or I eat. Caramel popcorn and Nanaimo bars, our family traditions. I also binge-watch *Grey's Anatomy*, dreaming of the day when I'm rushing around an emergency room and Leo is at our home, maybe preparing a late dinner. Just like Meredith and Derek, only Leo is even better looking than McDreamy.

I also spend way too much time on social media, creeping Leo, and Jada too. She just makes my blood boil with her posts. It's like Every. Single. Post. is about how great she is, and she's either in tight workout gear or her bathing suit, looking as if she's trying to be a model. Whatever. And she gets so many likes. Why? It's not like she's a celebrity.

And Leo is having the best time. I zoom in on every photo to look at the girls nearby, the ones in bikinis. There are a lot.

Some days I'm in bed all day, and other days I get my butt in gear and go to the gym. My gym visits only happen because I've looked at fit people on social media (like Jada with her hard abs and the girls in bikinis in Leo's posts) and know I'm getting fatter by the second. My parents bought me a six-month pass to the gym for Christmas. On the days I don't go work out it's because there's this heaviness that won't let me get out of bed. I've never felt like this before. Ever. It's like the mud I'm stuck in is sucking me in to my bed, not allowing me to move.

* * *

On the first day back after break, I catch up with Izzy in the halls. I've never been so thankful to be back at school before in my life. She has a bit of a suntan on her face, but with the raccoon eyes where she was probably wearing sunglasses or goggles.

"I feel like I haven't seen you in ages," I say.

She hugs me hard. "It has been ages. We need to catch up big-time."

"Yeah. We do. Felix back too?"

"Not until tomorrow." Izzy groans. "I miss him so much."

"Make up for lost time." I nudge her with my shoulder.

"Oh, yeah," she says. "How's life with Leo?"

I shrug. "He was gone too. Took a family vacay to Cancún. Some surprise Christmas gift from his parents. They left Christmas evening. So we also didn't see each other. But January will be better." Something jabs me inside. I want it to be better. *Please, make it better.*

"I heard there's a party this weekend," says Izzy.

"Yeah, I heard that too."

"Last semester of high school," says Izzy. "We gotta make it good."

"Yeah, let's do that," I say, trying to sound confident.

CHAPTER 17
PARTY TIME

Izzy gets ready for the party at my place.

"I don't know what to wear," I moan. I flop down on my bed and stare at the ceiling. "I ate like a pig over Christmas."

"For a start, get out of those sweats." Izzy is wearing tight jeans and a new powder-blue sweater that she got for Christmas. She stands in front of the mirror, putting on mascara.

"And what's wrong with my sweats?" I laugh. "I lived in them over the holidays."

She goes to my closet and rifles through it. "I can't believe your closet is actually colour-coded now. Is this something else you did over Christmas?"

"Yup. Took me one whole day."

She picks out a pair of dark jeans and throws them at me. They land on my face.

"And here's a sweater," she says. Another article of clothing lands on top of my stomach. It's pink.

"Okay, okay," I say. I get up off my bed and get dressed. I zip up the jeans, but they are a bit snug, like a-little-fat-rolling-over-the-top snug, and I have to squat to get them to loosen. "That darn caramel corn," I say to Izzy.

"And your mom's Nanaimo bars, I bet." She raises one eyebrow.

"Are there any left?"

"Are you kidding? I finished them off in, like, two days. And she and I actually made another batch. And I ate all the caramel corn and shortbread cookies. I had nothing else to do." I squat again.

Izzy puts on her winter jacket. "Let's roll," she says. Then she picks up her backpack. "You got booze?"

I nod.

From my place we truck through the snow to the subway station. Felix is meeting us there. Leo said he couldn't come because of an early swim time. His schedule is packed, as usual. I understand, but I want him by my side at the party, slow dancing, kissing, having fun.

The lights are all on at the house. I can see the bodies inside through the front window and know the parents must be gone. The last big party before everyone really starts cramming for first-semester exams. Without knocking, Izzy and I enter the house, and take off our boots at the front door. We weave through the bodies to head into the kitchen with our booze.

As soon as I walk into the kitchen, I see Leo, standing with a few of his friends. Red cup in hand. Laughing about something. Izzy nudges me. "Leo's here?" she whispers.

"Apparently," I reply.

"I thought he wasn't coming."

"That's what he told me."

She shrugs. "Probably changed his mind. No biggie."

Except it is to me. Why didn't he text to tell me? That's not hard to do. He's so busy talking to his friends that he hasn't seen me yet. What is happening to us?

"Go," says Izzy. "I'll make drinks."

I hand her my vodka bottle, and a can of soda. Then I walk over to Leo.

"Hey," I say. "You're here."

He turns and flashes his smile at me, but he doesn't reach out to hug me or even touch me. He shrugs. Then sips his drink. "It's our last semester of high school. Might as well make the most of it."

"Five months to go!" One of his friends holds up a red cup. He turns away from me. What was it I just saw in his eyes? Is he pulling away from me? Leo and his friends all cheer loudly. He can't be. He just can't be. I won't let that happen. We're supposed to be together.

Izzy shows up with our drinks and I hold mine up too. Now I can cheer and look as if I'm having fun when I'm actually feeling a little hurt. Well, a lot hurt.

"What are we toasting to?" Izzy asks. She takes a swig of her drink.

"The end of high school," says Leo. "And moving on to bigger and better things." He glances over at me but doesn't smile.

We all tap cups and I take a huge gulp. The booze burns my throat. Bigger and better things? Obviously, what is out there for him is something better than me. I take another big gulp. And another. And another. Is he pushing me aside? Why did he lie to me and tell me he couldn't come to the party?

Hours later, I'm up in the bathroom puking. Izzy holds my hair as I wretch over the toilet. "Oh shiiiiit," I slur. "I'm soooo drunk."

Izzy laughs. "How much did you drink?"

"Too much. Where's Leeeeo? He wouldn't dance with me. I tried to get him to, and he wouldn't. I'm still his girlfriend. He should want to dance with me. He should love me."

"Shhh," says Izzy. "He didn't dance with you because you're a little drunk, Nova."

"Where is he? Did he go home?"

"I think he's downstairs."

I stand up and reach for the sink to steady myself. In the

mirror, I see that my mascara is smudged. I try to wipe it.

"Let me do it," says Izzy. With a tissue, she cleans me up, and we head down the stairs. I hold the railing all the way down, and almost miss the bottom step. I right myself and laugh.

When my feet are firmly planted, I start my search for Leo. I stumble through the living room and ask a boy from my Math class, "Have you seen Leeeeeo?"

"You're wasted."

When I can't find Leo in the living room, I stagger to the kitchen. I need to hold on to the walls to keep my balance. He's not there either. I start to cry. Did he go home without saying goodbye? Why would he do that? Why wouldn't he say goodbye to me?

Then I see him through the kitchen window, standing on the outside deck with his coat on. He's out there with Jada. She's such a b-b-itch. I try and run to the door, feeling as if I have two left feet.

I hear someone say. "Nova's hammered."

I fling open the back door and a blast of cold air flows in.

"Leo," I call out. I start shivering.

I hear him say, "Nova?"

Then I hear one of his friends laugh and say, "She's gone. Like lit."

Then I hear Jada laugh and say, "She was puking in the bathroom upstairs."

Leo leaves his group of friends and comes over to me. He doesn't get close to me and I want him to. Instead, he stands by the railing and just stares at me. I want him to hug me, kiss me, go upstairs with me. We can now. We've already done it so it wouldn't matter. I would do that. I start to giggle. We could have a bobble-head audience and I wouldn't care. Noooooo, I wouldn't.

"Leeeeeo. Let's go upstairs. Have sehhhhx."

"Jeez, Nova." He takes a step toward me. "Not so loud." It's like he's whispering.

I hear someone from the distance. "Go upstairs, bro! FYI, she just puked."

"So what!" I yell back.

"Nova," says Leo quietly. "You're a mess. Shut the door."

"No, I'm nawwwwt." I cross my arms across my chest to stop shivering.

"Yeah, you are." He shakes his head at me.

"Shut the damn door!" Someone yells from inside the kitchen.

"Leeeo!" I stare at him. Why won't he come closer to me and kiss me? He used to love kissing me. I want him to kiss me. Now. Then I see Jada from a distance.

He gets a little closer and puts his hand on my elbow. "Go inside."

"Kiss me, Leo." I look up at him. He looks as if he has four eyes in my blurred vision.

"Nova, I think you should go home."

"Why? So . . . you . . . can . . . go upstairs with Jada?" I start to walk over to her, knowing I'm staggering, knowing I shouldn't, but not able to stop myself. "She's a boyfriend-stealing biiiitch!"

"Oh man, we're going to have a cat fight," says a guy. "I can't wait. My bet's on Jada. Nova's gonna swing and miss."

Leo grabs my arm and pulls me back. "Nova. Stop."

Suddenly, I'm crying. Tears just pouring down my face. "My mom is going to kill me."

"That's not my fault."

"It is your fault," I yell at him. "You didn't kiiiiiss me."

Leo holds up his hands. "I'm outta here."

Suddenly, Izzy and Felix are beside me. "Come on, Nova," says Izzy. "We're going to get you home. You're sleeping at my place tonight."

CHAPTER 18
SORRY, SORRY, SORRY

The next morning, I wake up with my head pounding, my stomach whirling and an ache in my heart. As soon as I plant my feet on the floor beside Izzy's bed, I run to the toilet and throw up. I come back to the bedroom and fall back on her queen-size bed.

"I wish I were a turtle so I could duck my head in my shell."

"You were pretty drunk." Izzy sits up, crawls over me and puts on a robe.

"Yeah. Let's not talk about it." I groan. "But . . . what did I do, Izzy?"

"Well, for starters, you got wasted."

"I hate Jada," I say.

"I used to think she was the problem, but I don't anymore." Izzy sits down beside me. "You and Leo are coming apart yourselves."

"How can I fix it?" The tears lurk again. Why am I always crying? I need to be tougher, and think of solutions, not wallow in tears. "It's like we had sex, and everything changed."

"You might want to apologize."

"I'm not apologizing to her."

"I didn't mean to Jada."

"Yeah, I know, I've got to apologize to Leo." I push myself up.

She stands and holds out her hand. "Come on. Get up. You got work to do."

Since I can't eat a thing, Izzy makes me a Vitamin C emergency drink, and puts it in a to-go cup. Before I leave, I take a quick shower, but even that doesn't help my hangover. As I walk to the subway, I puke in the trash can. Even though I feel awful, I know I need to call Leo. It goes to voicemail. Right. He's at the pool. So I text him to phone me when he has a moment and I add a heart emoji and the word *sorry* in caps.

I get home to an empty apartment and am instantly relieved that I don't have to go through the question period. I go to my room and crawl into bed, pulling the covers over my head. If I could delete last night, I would.

I don't get to talk to Leo until early afternoon when he calls me. My hands are shaking when I pick up the phone and I fumble with it, almost dropping it on the floor.

"Hey," I say after three rings. "I'm so sorry." The words push out of my mouth.

"Yeah, okay." He's curt.

"You mad at me?" My voice is a bit whiny.

"You were pretty drunk and said some things."

"I know." I pause. "I'm really sorry. I don't know what got into me."

"You weren't very nice to Jada."

I try and swallow. Is he defending her? Why would he do that? Since I don't want to start another fight, I say, "I'll apologize to her too." I pause before I say, "We good?"

"Sure," he says. "See you tomorrow."

I can't blame him for being cold with me. I was shrieking like a witch with a broom. I send a quick text to Jada saying sorry, then I pull the covers over my head again. And stay in bed for the rest of the day.

* * *

The week flies by. With exams creeping up on all of us, Leo and I eat lunch together but that's the extent of our get-togethers. He's busy with swimming and studying. I'm tutoring and studying. My tutoring hours have picked up, and I'm thankful for the extra distraction. My Grade Ten kids are nervous, so part of my job is to be encouraging.

On Friday, I see Leo in the hall. He stops. I reach for his hand. "Hey, missed you," I say quietly. I'm certainly not going to have a redo of my awful drunken night and say something mean to him.

He gives my hand a squeeze. Tingles spread from my hand to my heart. He still does that to me. I look up at him. "Does that mean you miss me too?"

"I've been so busy, Nova. It's hard to miss anyone."

A big ball of something lodges in my throat. My eyes sting. "I said I missed you," I whisper, "and you can't even tell me you miss me back. What is happening to us?"

"You're reading way too much into this. I need to get through these exams and I'm still swimming twice a day."

Am I reading too much into this? Is he right? A tear slides down my face. I swipe at it. What is wrong with me? I've cried more in the past few weeks than I have in years.

Leo glances up and down the hall before he turns back to me. "Jeez, Nova. Don't cry in the hall. Yes, I do miss you, but I'm so bloody busy with everything. And I do want to get a few good grades."

"I, I, can't help it. I just can't." And with that, I'm off and running down the school hall, my feet slapping the tiled floor. I head straight to the restroom.

I push open the door and find an empty stall, locking the door. As I sit down on the closed toilet seat, I cry. With my head in my hands, the tears just fall. It is not like me to cry over something so stupid, but my heart aches like someone is stabbing a knife into it. Over and over. I put my hand to my heart to feel it beating. What is happening between us?

I hear footsteps. Oh god. I wipe my eyes, knowing I need to pull it together. There's no way anyone can see me like this, and I can't miss Biology. It's the last class before exams and for sure we'll get some tips on what to study.

"Nova?" It's Izzy.

"What?" I sniffle.

She knocks on the stall I'm in. "Unlock the door."

I step out and Izzy stares at me. "Shit, girl. What's going on?"

"I dunno. Leo and I aren't doing so well."

"We're all under a lot of stress right now," she says. "Exams are making everyone uptight."

I nod. "Yeah. I know. It's hard to carve out time to see each other. But it seems like more than that."

"Maybe study together. You can help him."

"Why do you always have the best ideas?" I wipe under my eyes.

"I'm standing on the outside looking in," Izzy says. "Makes it easier." She grabs my hand and pulls me out of the bathroom stall. "Come on. Let's get to class."

"Do I look like I've been crying?" I ask her.

She pulls out a makeup bag. "Throw a bit on. You'll be fine."

I quickly put on some blush and lip gloss. I hand her back the bag. She links her arm in mine. "You look fabulous. Come on. Straight back."

I text Leo as we are walking down the hall.

Sorry. Uptight about exams. If u need help studying, let me know.

He texts back right away, giving me a checkmark emoji. My heart warms.

* * *

"How do you think you did?" I ask Leo after our biology exam.

Since I finished earlier than him, I waited outside the door of the exam room. He took the entire two hours to finish. For both of us, this is our last exam of the semester. January is almost done, and exams are finally over. We can all breathe. Now it's time to celebrate that we only have one semester left in our entire high school career. I'm so hoping Leo and I can go out somewhere tonight, even for a coffee, or to a movie, anything. Even a movie at my place. Time is just flying by. We're almost done high school. Are we almost done our time together too? I can't go there.

"I think I did okay," he says. He puts his arm around me and kisses my head as we walk down the hall. "Thanks to your help."

"My pleasure," I say, leaning into him, the quivers of love still there. This is how we used to be. "Should we celebrate somewhere?" I ask. "Even a movie at my place?"

"I don't have time," he says. "We've got a meet this weekend in Calgary. I'm flying out tomorrow."

I pull away from him. "You're going to Calgary? You didn't tell me that."

He takes his arm off my shoulder and shoves his hands in the pockets of his jacket. "You were so stressed about studying, I didn't want to add to it."

I stop walking, grab his jacket sleeve, and make him turn toward me. I stare up at him, into his eyes. I see his Adam's apple move up and down as he inhales and exhales, as if he's bracing himself for what I have to say. I don't want to fight with him again. Maybe I should just kiss him, here in the hallway.

But then I can't control myself and the words fly out of my mouth. "What kind of relationship do we have if you can't tell me things?"

He blows out that air, heaves a huge sigh and runs his hand through his hair. "Not this again, Nova."

"What do you mean? 'Not this again'?" Something inside me is lit on fire, and I can't seem to stop it from burning. I always seem to be the bad person in our fights. Everything is always my fault. I don't want to fight with him, but this makes me mad. Why wouldn't he tell me he wasn't going to be here for the weekend? Our one weekend with no commitments. Except he has HUGE commitments. I should understand. I should. And I do. But I'm hurt he didn't tell me.

"If I'd have told you and you did crappy on an exam, you'd blame me," he says. "So I didn't tell you and now I'm the bad guy for not telling you. I can't please you, Nova."

"I wouldn't have done poorly on an exam," I say snottily. "I've got more focus than that." How dare he say that to me? "I am the top senior student, academically. You know that, right?"

He holds up his hands. "I can't win with you." He starts backing up.

"You're going to leave. In the middle of this discussion."

"It's not a discussion. You're pissed. I didn't tell you to protect you."

"To protect me? Um, for the record, I'm the one who got into U of T on early acceptance."

He shakes his head at me. "I know that. I said congrats. And I've said thank you for all the help you gave me."

"You should have told me. I wouldn't have *bombed* a test because of you." I stand ramrod still.

"I'm sorry," he says. "I really am."

Suddenly, I go all mushy inside and it's like the fire was put out with a heavy dose of water. He genuinely looks sorry. And now I'm genuinely sorry too. My emotions are like a roller coaster ride. Since I'm not angry anymore, I step toward him. "I'm sorry too."

He doesn't hug me. Instead, he avoids eye contact and says, "I should go. I gotta pack." He turns and walks away from me.

As I watch him walk away, I want to collapse on the floor and shrivel into a ball.

CHAPTER 19
LONELY

With Leo out of town, Izzy and I head to the gym on Saturday. It's one of the few free weekends we get, where exams are done and the new semester is yet to begin, so there is no homework to do. Nothing. I would have loved to have Leo home so we could do something fun together, but obviously that's not going to happen.

Once again, I try and up my weights in my workout. My body is starting to show the effects, is starting to bulk up, or that's what I keep telling myself when my clothes don't fit.

After our workout, we decide to get some food at the community centre concession stand. As much as I try to tell the woman at the counter that I want a salad, I order a burger. Izzy gets a coffee and pastry.

"That's all you're having?" I ask her.

"Felix and I have a dinner date tonight," she says. "To celebrate exams being over."

"Ooh-la-la. Where are you guys going?" We sit down at an empty table. I am happy for her, I truly am, even though I have this intense loneliness that my boyfriend isn't here, or available to take me for dinner.

"Felix found an Indian restaurant that he says is as good as some of the places in London. Apparently, they're well known. He says it's a hole in the wall, cheap and the food is authentic."

"Cool," I say. "You guys are still hot and heavy."

"He's a good guy."

I take a break from shoving food in my mouth to look at her. "What are you going to do when this year is over, though?"

Her eyes light up. "We've got a plan," she says. The excitement in her voice is real. Brimming. Like it might spill over. I wish it would spill over on to me and give me some much-needed energy.

"Give me the goods," I say. "You know me, I like plans."

"I might take a gap year and go live in London." She does this little shake with her shoulders. "I can get a work permit and get a job." She almost squeals.

"You might live in London, England? Wow, Izzy. That's so fantastic. So exotic."

"Yeah, why not?" Izzy says. "It'd be fun for a year. Get to know the city. Visit Buckingham Palace." She laughs.

"That is so cool." I sit back. I'm hoovering my burger and fries like a vacuum cleaner sucking up crumbs. "That sounds so, almost surreal."

"You can come visit me." Her eyes twinkle.

"Yeah, sure, maybe." I take another bite.

She points to my plate. "You ate that burger like you've never eaten before."

I push the empty plate off to the side. "Stress eating," I say.

"You and Leo that bad, eh?"

I nod. "We had a fight before he left for some swim meet in Calgary that he didn't tell me about. I don't know what's wrong with me. I keep picking at him."

Izzy sits forward and clasps her hands together. "I know you don't want to hear this but . . . maybe it's time you guys broke up."

Just thinking about the word *breakup* makes my heart whack

against my T-shirt. *Whack. Whack. Whack.* It hurts to beat like that. Really hurts. I shake my head. "No," I say. "We just need some time together to work things out."

"Why are you hanging on?" Izzy asks this gently.

"I love him." I turn the empty plate around and around.

"Do you really?"

"Yes," I say. "I do. Every time I think of not being with him, my heart aches so much I can barely breathe."

"Are you guys going to the Valentine's Day dance?"

I nod. "I think so. We talked about it when they announced it, but we haven't talked about it since." I glance at Izzy. "Are you and Felix going?"

"Oh, yeah. Felix is all pumped for a Canadian high school dance. Like it's some novelty. We should go together. The four of us."

"Sounds like a plan."

Valentine's Day is the perfect time to get us back on track.

CHAPTER 20
MYSTERY VISIT

"Try something on for me," says Izzy.

I'm rifling through my closet of clothes. I don't own a ton of dresses as they're kind of not my thing. "Are you wearing a dress?"

Valentine's Day is tomorrow, and so is the dance. Izzy sits on my bed, her back leaning against the pillows. We went shopping earlier and I bought a beautiful, love-themed card for Leo and a chocolate heart filled with his favorite Swiss chocolates, and she got Felix a funny card and some weird, plush bear.

At the beginning of the week, the dance committee put up red-and-white Valentine's Day dance posters all over the school. Leo and I haven't talked too much about the dance, but I assume we're going. It was something we talked about back in January and he seemed excited about. And he's not out of town, and his swim practice ends at six. I know that because I asked him for his schedule, which he did sort of give to me, reluctantly. I thought if I had his schedule, we wouldn't have to fight about him leaving. I would know and be prepared.

Now I have the big decision about what to wear to the dance. I want to look good for him, so we can slow dance and make out on the dance floor, preferably in front of Jada.

"I'm not sure what I'm wearing," Izzy says. "Well, probably

not a dress. But . . . def a skirt and booties. I just have to figure out which one."

"Are you doing the Valentine's Day colour thing?"

Izzy shakes her head. "Nah. I'm not into that. Although Felix wants to wear a red tie."

I keep going through my clothes and pull out a little skirt I wore for Christmas dinner. It's black and gold and short. I could match it with black tights and black boots. Or even heels. I own one pair of black heels. My feet might kill by the end of the night, though. I hold it up for Izzy's approval.

"Yeah," she says, nodding. "That's perfect. You could pair it with a black blouse or even just a simple black T-shirt. Put it on."

"It's not red or pink, though," I say.

"Whatever." Izzy makes a circular motion with her fingers. "Let me see."

I slip it over my head, and down to my hips. I reach behind to do up the zipper, and it's a squeeze. It barely does up at the back, and I feel as if I'm going to pop the zipper if I move. It's one of my bigger skirts too.

"Suck it in." Izzy laughs.

"Ohmygod," I say, holding my breath. "It's all that weight lifting." I manage to get it done up, but the clasp won't close.

"Don't forget about the hamburgers and fries." Izzy throws a pillow at me.

"Shut up." I throw back.

"I don't think it works," she says. "It's a little tight and I don't think you'll be comfortable all night. You got anything else you can wear? Something flowier, looser?"

"What are you saying?"

"Nothing. I just think it's a little tight. You'll lose it. I wouldn't stress."

"How could I have let this happen? I bet it's the pill."

Izzy shrugs. "Might be. It's made your boobs bigger, though, so that's a good thing. That's what happened to Sara. She went on it and her boobs got huge. Lucky. Wish that would have happened to me. Find something to give you cleavage."

"Lucy too," I say. "She's always wearing low-cut shirts to show them off."

I find a summer floral dress that has short sleeves instead of spaghetti straps. It's not light floral and has oranges and blues, so it could work. I hold it up for Izzy. "Too summery?" I ask.

"Pair it with a jacket."

I slip the dress on. Since it does have a V-neck, I have cleavage.

"That's looks fantastic." She pauses for a second before she says, "Maybe we should do more cardio at the gym. It burns the calories."

"I've kinda got my period too and I feel bloated." I put a hand on my stomach. Then I look at her because something about that last comment doesn't make sense. "Why are you reading up on that stuff about burning calories? You don't have an ounce to lose."

She shrugs and sheepishly looks away. Then she turns back to me and says, "What do you mean you *kind of* have your period? You still getting those ones that last all of a day?"

"Half a day sometimes. I'm not complaining," I say.

"Maybe you should see a doctor, Nova. Your body isn't adjusting to the pill. Maybe go off it and try some other form of contraception."

"Maybe we should just do condoms." I throw the dress on the bed and hurriedly put my oversized T-shirt back on. "Or we could do nothing with the amount I see Leo these days."

My phone beeps and Izzy picks it up off my night table,

reading the screen. "Speaking of Leo," she says, tossing me the phone. I catch it in my hand and read his text.

Can I come over?

"He wants to come over," I say to Izzy. "Weird. He doesn't usually just pop by. He knows my parents are gone, though." My heart races. "Finally, maybe we can be together. It's been ages." I clap my hands. "Pick out something for me to wear that won't make me look fat."

She hops off my bed, goes to my closet and picks out a long shirt. "Wear this with tights. I'll head. Go for it."

I send him back a heart emoji.

Within thirty minutes, Izzy is gone, and Leo is at my apartment door. I've made my bed, so it has no creases, and I've lit all the candles. I've even made us a little snack of cheese and crackers for after. I answer the door and the first thing I say is, "We've got the place to ourselves." I almost sing my words, and pull him in, shutting the door. Then I wrap my arms around him and try to kiss him. But he steps away from me.

"Don't, Nova."

I frown and take a step back. "What's up?"

"I need to talk to you." He stands in the entrance to my apartment and doesn't take his shoes or coat off. He looks . . . nervous or something. His hands are twitching by his side. Weird. His eyes don't have their usual sparkle, and his mouth is one straight line, no smile. No happy-to-see-you look on his face. He seems to be looking at everything but me, his eyes darting side to side.

"About what?" I ask. "Is something wrong?"

"I don't know how to say this without hurting you, but . . ." He runs his hands through his hair, and he lets out huge exhale. My feet are rooted to my spot on the floor. I don't speak.

Without hurting me. I don't like the sound of this.

"Um," he tries to continue. He hesitates for a brief second before he blurts out, "I think we should break up. I didn't want to do it by text."

I stare at him. Just stand there and stare. My throat is parched. My lips suddenly feel cracked and dry. I feel as if a ball of something is stuck in the middle of my throat, clogging it so I can't speak. I cough to make it move, clear it out of there.

Then I blurt out, "You're, uh, you're, breaking up with me?" I shake my head, back and forth. "The day . . . before Valentine's Day?"

He swallows. I can see that his neck is red, his face too. "Nova, I'm so sorry," he says. "I can't do this anymore."

"We've got . . . months left before you have . . . to go."

"I'm just not . . . feeling it anymore. We fight all the time. It's not fun. I want to be free for these last months of high school. Have a good time."

"Free?" I suck in a breath. "Do you want to be *free* to be with other people?"

Leo shoves his hands in his pockets. "It's not that. Just be free to have fun. Do what I want. Not always have to think about getting together with you."

Blood rushes to my head. My body is numb, cold. "Are you seeing Jada?"

"This has nothing to do with her?"

"Did you have sex with her too? You did, didn't you!"

"Nova, don't do this. Jada's not the reason. I've never had sex with her. We're the reason. All we do is fight. All the time. I'm sick of it."

"Sick of it? You sound as if I've put you in prison or something."

"You've got to admit that —"

"— that what?" I cut him off. "That you had sex with me and now you . . . want . . . to dump me. Did you just get what you wanted from me?"

"No. That's not why, Nova," he says. "It's the fighting. It makes me tired and I . . . can't do it anymore. There's this lack of connection between us. And not sexual connection. Just connection."

"Get out!" The words fly out of my mouth. I move toward him and pound on his chest. "How could you do this before Valentine's Day?"

He grabs my hands. "Nova, don't be like this."

"Don't be like what?"

"You know as well as I do, that we aren't good." He opens the door. "I can't do this."

The tears start cascading down my face. "I love you, Leo."

"I have to go. I'm sorry."

"Did you hear me?! I love you!"

The door shuts and I stand still. Then I collapse to the floor and sob.

CHAPTER 21
SMASHED HEART

The smashed chocolate heart box I bought for Leo stares me in the face the next morning. Tears stream down my face. Leo broke up with me. *He broke up with me.*

I told him I loved him, and he left.

I look around my room at the cracker box, the taco chip bag and the cookie box, all of them empty. I grab the taco chip bag and crinkle it in my hands before I stuff it in my trash can. Then I step on the cookie box, smashing it flat and stuff it into the trash as well. And the cracker box. But it's the heart box that makes me boil inside, red and shiny, and . . . empty. I ate all the chocolates. I give it a good twist with my foot. Then it also goes in the trash. I rip up the beautiful card I bought him, and signed with a heartfelt message, into tiny pieces.

I wipe my face.

Stop crying. Just stop.

My mom is in the kitchen drinking coffee when I walk in. I stayed in my room last night, and she left me alone because she thought I was studying. I'm wearing my grey sweats and a big sweater and zero makeup. Whatever.

"Happy Valentine's Day!" She hands me a card and a bag of red candy hearts. She gives me the same thing every year because I love the hearts.

"Thanks, Mom." I croak out the words.

I open the card and read the caption.

To a Special Daughter on Valentine's Day!

The card goes on in Hallmark fashion to tell me how great I am. Then at the bottom is my mother's handwriting.

Nova, I'm so proud of you! You're going to go on to do amazing things with your life. I'm so glad you're going to the university of your dreams! You will make the world's finest doctor!

"Thanks, Mom." I keep staring at her handwriting. I think I want to keep this card. My mother isn't exactly the Hallmark card-type person, so this is a big stretch for her. Plus, the card is also reminder that I can and will do things. With or without a stupid boyfriend.

"You're welcome. I mean every word," she says.

"It's great." I keep looking at it so I don't have to make eye contact with her. She might figure out something is wrong.

"You and Leo have plans for Valentine's Day?"

And then it happens. The tears are there again, burning the hell out of my eyeballs. I thought I'd cried them all out last night. I go to the fridge and get out some cheese, cutting myself a huge hunk. "I'm not sure. I think he's swimming," I say to answer her question. Then I say, "We need to put crackers on the grocery list."

I don't know why I don't tell her, but I don't. Maybe I just don't want to hear the words, "we broke up" come out of my mouth. I don't want to make it official. I don't want to believe it's true.

"Oh, that's too bad. It doesn't matter. It's just one day."

To deflect the conversation off me, I ask, "What about you and Dad?"

My mother laughs. "Valentine's Day is long gone for us."

I glance at her. "You guys seem pretty distant from each other."
Then for some reason I blurt out, "Why don't you just divorce?"

She stares at me. "Where is that coming from?" Her eyebrows
almost touch, she's frowning so much. "Your father and I might
be going through a difficult time, but that's not the option for us.
We'll work through this."

"Mom," I say. "You're in denial about you and Dad. You guys
don't have a relationship."

"Honey, it's marriage. We've hit a hard place, but we'll work
to bring it back."

Unlike Leo who didn't want to work at *us*. No. He just wanted
to be *free*. I shake my head at her. "Every night you're in different
rooms. Dad spends all his time on the balcony with his whisky
and you run around trying to make the marriage look real. When
clearly it's not."

She doesn't say anything back. There's this look on her face of
sadness or something. Maybe even hurt. Sort of how I feel inside.
Sad. Hurt. All of those emotions are sitting underneath my skin.
Am I putting my pain on her?

Finally, she says, "I'm sorry you feel that way." She stands
straight, her back like a pin. "We're working on some things. This
has been an extremely tough time for your dad. He lost a job he
liked. And Brad has really hurt him."

"Brad is fine and not the problem." Why I keep throwing
stuff at her is beyond me, but I can't help myself. My words are
tumbling out of my mouth before I can stop them.

"His lack of communication is really hard for your dad and
me. This isn't about the money."

"You put a lot of pressure on him to succeed."

She does her *almost* sigh. "Maybe we did." Her answer

surprises me, as she is usually so defensive. Maybe his absence at Christmas has made her think.

She looks at me and gives a little smile. "I will agree with you. Dad and I both realize that we were hard on him. But . . . we could have helped him. To use your word, he was in *denial* that anything was wrong. He didn't trust us." She pauses before she says. "It's Valentine's Day and I'd love to tell him I love him and not by text." She turns away from me and starts washing the breakfast dishes.

Suddenly I feel horrible for saying anything about a divorce, and her relationship, and for talking about Brad. She turns to stare at me, and now her eyes are filled with tears. "I hope you have a great Valentine's Day."

This morning, the day after Leo broke up with me, I can't handle *her* tears. I walk toward the door. "Yeah, you too. I better get to school," I mumble.

As I walk to the subway station, I know I was a bit mean to her. I fire her off a text with a heart emoji. I will go to school, focus on this new semester. I will get good grades and be that top student in senior year. That's going to be my new goal. Forget boyfriends. I don't want a marriage like my mother. I want to make something of my life.

As I'm waiting for my train, I text Brad.

Phone Mom, please. She does love you. Oh, and Happy Valentine's Day!

At least I can try to make something right.

* * *

All day, I check the halls before walking down them. I. Do. Not. Want. To. See. Leo. Everyone is talking about the dance and giving out those hokey Valentine's Day cards you buy at the grocery store. Others are wearing pink and red. And then there's those who don't like the day, so they wear black. I want none of it, so I'm wearing grey. If I had my choice, I'd rip every poster off the wall and tear it into shreds.

But I don't. Instead, I walk the halls alone, my hair hanging in front of my face, hoping to hide from everyone. I avoid making eye contact. I slip into every class like I'm invisible. And I ignore the whispers around me. I hardly even talk to Izzy, and when she asks me to go to lunch with her and Felix, I say no. I eat my lunch in the far corner of the library. Since I have Calculus this semester, I work on equations and eat and don't look up. Fortunately, I don't have any tutoring today, so when school is done, I can go home and hide in my bedroom. The talk around me is nonstop Valentine's Day, and I can't stand it, and the red and pink everyone is wearing is nauseating.

I manage to get through my classes and, finally, it's last class of the day. The one I'm dreading. Leo is in Chemistry with me. I contemplate going home, skipping class, but then I think about that. I'm the one with the good marks. Me. Why should I have to be the one to not go to class? I will suck it up and ignore him.

I am almost at the door to the class when I see him with Jada. My insides boil. Like hot lava that wants to erupt. Without thinking about any type of consequence, I storm over to them.

"You are such a liar," I hiss. I'm erupting and I know it, but I can't stop myself.

"Nova, it's not what you think."

"And how do you know what I think?"

I turn and glare at Jada. "You're pathetic." I want to rip her face apart. "You can't get your own boyfriend, so you have to take mine!"

I hear someone say, "Uh oh, Nova's losing it!"

"Cat fight!"

I rush into the lab and sit down. My entire body is shaking, and I can feel sweat dripping down my back. Leo comes in to class, and I don't look at him, or anyone, for that matter. I stare down at the periodic table I have taped to the inside of my notebook. The teacher comes in and I turn my attention to inert gases.

At the end of class, I bolt out of the room. The energy in the hall is all about the stupid, stupid, stupid dance. I rush down the hall to my locker. I grab my coat, slam my locker and head to the front door, running as fast as I can.

PART THREE

MAY 9

Blue-and-red lights flash in the darkened sky when I arrive back where I left her. I'm gasping, my heart whacking against my chest, I've run so fast. My entire body aches; sharp, shooting pains hit my stomach, but I must ignore the pain. I duck into the trees. I stiffen up completely, holding my breath now, as I watch the policewoman walk over to an ambulance.

Is she in there? Are they helping her?

Is she breathing?

I know I should show myself, own up to what I did. I should. My feet won't move. Have I run all this way for nothing, just to hide in the bushes? I want to phone Brad again. But I can't. He would tell me to move, show my face and admit what I've done.

"Go out there. Go out there now. Make it right. Find out if she's okay," I talk to myself, muttering.

But I stay behind the bushes. A paramedic comes out of the ambulance and talks to the policewoman. The policewoman glances around as if she's looking for someone. Me. She's looking for me. I'm the one who did this.

Go. Get out there.

Should I?

The paramedic shuts the door of the ambulance, gets in and suddenly the siren rips through the air. And it's gone. Gone. Is she that bad that they need to race her to a hospital? Does that mean she's not dead? Dying? What?

The lights of the police car seem to throb at the same speed as my heart beats. The policewoman glances around again, as does the fireman. He points to the front entrance. Then he holds up his hands as if to say, "I don't know."

You can do this, Nova. You can do this. *I push the bushes aside.*

And step out. I slowly walk toward the policewoman and the fireman.

They turn and see me.

"Did I kill her?" I ask.

CHAPTER 22
THE MARCH BEFORE MAY

It's another Friday. And another weekend looming in front of me. Another boring weekend. I get out of bed and put on, once again, my sweats. They're like my lifeline, and I've worn them to school for a month now. Every. Day. I have two pairs and I rotate them. I enter the kitchen and my mother eyes me up and down. I shove a McDonald's paper bag in the blue recycling bin.

Leo and I have been officially broken up for a month and I'm still throwing-things angry and crying-in-the-shower sad. Sometimes I sit on my bed and rock with my starfish necklace in my hand. Leo gave it to me on my birthday, that first night we had sex. Every day I tell myself to get over it, but something inside of me won't let go. The weather doesn't help. March is like this month of wet, slushy snow that makes the world look dirty. Streetcars screech on the tracks, people trek through the slush and the sky is grey. Like me. I'm grey. I can't seem to find any light anywhere in my world. My only glimmer of hope is my high average in my studies, the tests I get back that show that I'm successful at something. Because I'm sure not successful in the relationship department. Every night, I shut my door and work. I redo essays if I see one mistake.

And I certainly haven't gone out. I just don't feel like going anywhere with anybody. Even Izzy. Although she tries.

"You have nicer clothes in your closet," says my mother.

"I'm all for comfort, Mom."

"Did you go get takeout again last night?"

"I did."

"What time?"

I shrug. "I dunno. Like, midnight."

"We bought you that gym pass for Christmas. Are you using it?"

I shrug again. "Sometimes. I like lifting weights." I've been going to the gym now and again but putting on gym clothes is a challenge. I wear sweats, like the ones I laughed at Izzy for wearing, what seems like ages ago. I want the year to end. I want high school and all its dramatics over.

"Are you okay?" My mother does have a concerned look on her face. I can't let it penetrate me, get beneath my skin. She's asked me this a lot. It's getting old.

"My marks are great," I say. "I'm studying a lot. That should make you happy."

"Nova, this isn't about me being happy. It's about you. I want you to be happy."

"I can't be happy. Leo doesn't want me."

"I'm so sorry, Nova. I think it's for the best, though."

"You know, I read an article about what to say when people are grieving, and that's something you should never say." I glare at her.

She tries to smile at me. "I haven't seen Izzy lately." Her voice has this high, chipper pitch to it, like it's fake, and she's just trying to cheer me up.

"She's got a boyfriend."

I fill a to-go cup with coffee and grab a banana. There's a pastry shop on my way to school and I stop there every morning and get this cheese bread that makes me happy. For a minute, anyway. Until I eat the last crumb. Then I'm sad again. And mad that I ate it. Just add that one to my list of feeling all the bad feels.

"I've got a tutoring session after school," I say without so much as glancing her way, "so I won't be home until five."

"I'm off at five too," she says. "I have the day off tomorrow. Did you want to do something?"

"Like what?" I stare at the tiles on the floor.

"Maybe we could go for a hike."

"A hike? Since when do you hike?" I shake my head. "We can talk about it later."

I leave the apartment and get on the elevator with some woman who has a kid screaming in a stroller. She is rocking the stroller back and forth, trying to get the baby to quiet down. I yank out my phone and go to a social media site. I start scrolling. Then I see something and it's like a rock has blasted through the elevator ceiling and landed on me. It's a photo on Jada's social media site. I can't stop staring at it. She's sitting on Leo's lap! They're kissing. Kissing! I close my eyes to the pain hitting my chest. The kid screams louder. The elevator hits ground. I let the woman get out first, helping her with her stroller. My entire body trembling.

I get outside and check the photo again. Why does she have to rub it in my face? I zip up my jacket and hurry to the subway. Once on, and seated, my shoulder up against the side of the train, I check Leo's profile. He doesn't post a lot, but every so often he puts something up. He has posted! It's a photo of him with a few of his club swim team friends. I exhale. Not the same photo. Guess who's lurking along the side, though? Jada! I shove my phone in my pocket.

When I get to school, I head right to class. Head down. Walking fast. With the new semester, I only have Izzy in one class of mine, and it's an elective. I see her and sit in the seat in front of her.

"Hey," she says.

"Jada posted a photo again," I mutter.

"Nova, stop. Let it go. You have to."

"I can't. They're kissing in it. And she posted it. Why would she do that?"

Suddenly, tears spring from my eyes. I'm so sick of crying but tears just seem to show up at the most random times. It's been weeks of tears. Weeks. No . . . a month. Exactly a month today. A flipping month of tears. I try to wipe them away with the back of my hand so no one can see. The word spread around the school that I'd got dumped. Jada flew in like a bird to perch on Leo's back. People talk about me, I know. I've heard the whispers. They even call me *Sweatpants Chick*. If they see me crying, this will get to Leo in a nanosecond. I'd run from the room, but I don't want to miss class. I must keep my marks in the high nineties.

"You okay?" Izzy asks softly.

I straighten my shoulders. "I'm fine."

"Let's go for a coffee after school today. Like we used to." Izzy presses her hands together as if she's praying. "Pleeeease. We can talk about this."

"I've got to tutor after school today," I say.

"Pretty pleeeeeease."

Izzy has stuck by me, tried to help. I know that. "I could go at five."

"Promise."

"Promise," I reply. It's coffee. That's monumental.

The class starts and I listen intently. The time flies by. It always does when I'm in class, because I can forget about everything if I listen to the lesson. But then it's over, and I have to go out in the hall again. Izzy walks out with me, but when we hit the fork, I go one way and she goes the other. As I'm pushing open the door to hit the stairwell to the second floor, I hear Leo's voice. He's coming down the stairs with Jada. I duck under the stairwell, and hide against the wall, sucking in everything to make myself as small as possible. Which lately, with takeout every night, isn't all that easy.

"We should go to Theo's after practice today." It's Jada.

"Sure," says Leo. "My favourite restaurant."

That was our place! We went there all the time. Leo and me. Why would they go there? Anywhere else but there. I can taste the hummus, smell the sizzling chicken. Leo loves their salad and souvlaki. I stand still. I hold my breath. Then they stop. They don't talk. But I hear them. I know they're kissing. My ears burn. Finally, I hear them go out the door. I run up the stairs and to my next class.

* * *

After school, I make some money tutoring a Grade Nine boy who struggles in math. Every week, we talk math and sports. He's on a hockey team and that's his focus, but he also wants to do well in school to keep options open, so I get that.

Because of Leo.

The boy reminds me of a younger Leo. Was this what he was like in grade nine? I remember all the girls drooling over Leo, and then he picked me. Me. And then he dumped me. Me.

The boy blinks as he looks at the equation. I show him a couple of steps to make it easier. He nods, like he gets it. Just like Leo used to. I'm the one who went through all Leo's applications with him, and helped him study, and encouraged him, and I still remember the day he signed. It was in the summer. We went to

Theo's afterward to celebrate. The boy scribbles down numbers, trying to get the answer. Now he's going to Theo's with her.

I want to cry. Again. *Get it together, Nova.*

I finish my tutoring session and immediately check my phone. Izzy has texted me five times, asking if we're still meeting for coffee. I say yes and tell her to pick the place. She picks a trendy café called Dark Horse.

Since it's not too far, I decide to walk, even though the streets are dirty slush. As I'm moving like a sloth to meet Izzy, I pass by Theo's restaurant. Why didn't I take the subway? I could have passed this without having to see it and be reminded of all that isn't. I stop. Suddenly, my throat dries, and I feel this tightness in my chest. Leo's swim practice would be from four to six and they will probably get here by six thirty.

Keep moving, Nova.

My feet move, but they feel as if they have weights on them. When I get to the café, Izzy has already ordered me a latte.

"Hey, thanks," I say. I sit down.

"So good to spend time with you," she says.

"You didn't have to buy. I'm making some good tutoring money." I don't look her in the eyes.

"My treat. Nova, I'm just happy to see you." She reaches across the table and grabs my hand. "How are you?"

"I'm okay." I pull my hand away.

"No really. Talk to me."

"I hate her so much," I say.

"Nova. I get it. But you have to let go of that hate."

"I know." I hang my head. "I can't seem to stop hating her, though."

"You've got so much going for you."

"Like what?"

"You're killing your grades. And you're going to be a doctor one day. Don't forget about you."

I shake my head. "And I'm fat. So there's that too."

"You can do this," urges Izzy.

"But it's so hard. It's all inside me and I just can't get it out. I've never hated anyone, but I hate her. And I hate him. And I hate seeing them together. It makes me feel crazy inside. I try to let go and it all comes rushing back." I pause before I say, "First the photo. Then . . . I heard them kissing in the stairwell. I knew they were because *we* used to do that. I had sex with him, and everything changed. It's been the worst day ever."

"Let's go shopping tomorrow."

"Shopping?" I roll my eyes. "Um, I think this body isn't a shopping body."

"Okay, then let's go to the gym."

"God, you're like my mother. She wants me to go on a hike with her." I pause for a second. Then I say, "They're going to Theo's tonight. Theo's! That's where we always used to go."

She stares at me. Deep. "Have you thought of seeing someone?"

"What? Like a shrink?"

"Even a doctor. Or a counsellor at school."

"You want me to talk to a guidance counsellor? Word would spread to all my teachers. The only place I feel normal is in class. My grades have never been better." I stand up. "Why did I even come here? You don't listen to me. You just want to lecture me. I can't help how I feel."

I grab my jacket and leave.

CHAPTER 23
BEING ALONE

As much as I know that I should walk right by Theo's, I don't. I stand in front of the sign, thinking about our first date and how happy we were. How he put a piece of souvlaki on his fork and passed it across the table for me to eat. How he waited to see my expression. "It's the most tender chicken I've ever had," he'd said. It was our place. It was a new place that opened up, a hole in the wall. But we loved it. How could he take her to our place?

So, no, I don't walk right by.

How long I stand there, I have no idea. But I can't move.

Go home, Nova. Go home.

I don't listen to the little voice of reason in my head. I see this big clump of bushes off to the side, and instead of going home, I move toward them, pushing the branches aside to get deep into them. I squat down, and after a few minutes, my thighs are in pain. So I kneel. But little stones dig into my kneecaps. How long I squat, kneel, sit, squat again, kneel again, sit . . . I don't know. But I don't leave. I can't. I wait. And wait.

Then I hear the voices. What am I doing? Why am I doing this? I peer through the branches and watch Leo and Jada walk toward the restaurant. Her arm is linked with his and she's leaning her head up against his upper arm. He's smiling down at her like he used to do with me. I get out my phone and take a photo. Then I take another. Then he stops to kiss her, and I get a perfect photo of them.

They go in the restaurant, and I stand up. I glance at the photo. I want to draw pictures on it. Horns. A witch's hat. I want to write the word *slut* on there. What if I doctored it up? Superimposed some other images on their heads, played around with it and put it on the internet for everyone to see that he was a jerk and she was a boyfriend-stealing bitch. With that idea planted firmly in my mind, I stuff my phone in my pocket and step out from behind the bushes.

All the way home, I think about what I'm going to do with the photos. I could put an . . . an animal head of some sort on her. The ugliest animal I can find.

I decide to ride the subway for the few stops to my dingy apartment.

I sit by myself, body pressed against the cold side of the train. I stare out the window at the grey world, concrete block after concrete block. I could also get a photo of Jada in the change room and post that online too. It seems so mean but . . . she was mean to me. She deserves it. Another stab hits my heart. They went to Theo's! I should be the one sitting across from Leo. It was me. Now it's her. The subway comes up for air, I get off at my stop and walk toward my apartment building.

I go by the church and the fire station. The church is dark for the night, but the fire station is lit right up. A garage door screeches, and I watch it rise, then suddenly a fire truck comes barrelling out. It turns on to the road and the siren starts. Off it goes.

Suddenly, it hits me that I am thinking like a crazy person. This is not me. I don't want to be the mean girl who posts terrible photos on the internet.

But she was a mean girl to you!

It's the inner voice again, only this time I listen. It's like I have twins inside of me. One bad, one good.

I keep walking, but much slower. My entire body feels thick and heavy. And I almost feel detached from it. I feel as if I'm underwater, drowning. When I swam, I had moments where I couldn't breathe. That's how I feel. There is an ache inside of me that just won't go away, and it gets worse and worse day after day. Instead of better. I want to lie on my bed and listen to country songs that talk about broken hearts. And cry.

My phone beeps. Once. Twice. Three times. I pull it out. Izzy has sent at least ten messages. Why did I run out on her? She's been so kind and patient with me. She's been nice to me and I treated her awfully.

I text her back.

I'm sorry.

I'm sorry too. I'm coming over.

I want to be alone thx though.

CHAPTER 24
BAD IDEA

At my mother's insistence, I get out of bed the next day and go to the gym. I have to make myself, plus, her nagging is insufferable. I told her I didn't want to go for a stupid hike. So she insisted I go to the gym. Instead of wearing spandex, I opt for sweatpants. Maybe they'll make me sweat more, which might help me lose the weight I'm gaining from eating my way through my evenings.

The entire time I'm riding the stationary bike, the vision of Jada and Leo in a lip-lock burns my eyeballs. He used to put his hands all over my body, and now he does the same thing with her. Maybe I need to get an awful photo of her and post it instead. But what? I pedal and pedal and think and think.

Then it hits me.

Does he have sex with her at school in the same hidden hall we went to? We only did it once there, but who knows how many times they've been there. The thought makes me want to vomit. *Come Monday morning, I'm going to put my sleuthing skills in action.* I get off the bike and wipe the sweat off my face with my oversized T-shirt. I've got a goal.

In the change room, after the workout, I'm stripping down when I hear my name.

"Nova!" I look over and see Izzy. "I was hoping I'd catch you here."

"Hey," I say. I find it a bit convenient that she's here the same time as me. "You here with Felix?"

I see this sheepish look on her face. "No," she says.

"Did my mother tell you I was here?"

"She's worried about you, Nova." Izzy tilts her head and I can see her gaze taking in my fat body.

I quickly wrap my towel around my torso. "Why are you looking at me like that?" I ask her.

"Nothing." Izzy turns from me, but it doesn't matter because I saw the shocked look on her face. With my shampoo bag in hand, I go to the private shower area instead of the open one.

When I'm done, I return to the area of the change room where I put my clothes and Izzy is still sitting on the bench, waiting for me. I get dressed in clean sweats. Without talking, Izzy and I head out to the lobby of the community centre.

"I'm starving," she says. "You wanna grab something to eat?"

"The way you looked at me, I probably shouldn't eat." I know my shoulders cave forward. I stare at the floor, and not her.

"Nova, come on. I'm sorry for yesterday. Let's sit and talk."

"As long as you don't judge me."

"I won't judge you. I worry about you, and your head space."

"Don't worry about me." We find a table and drop our backpacks down before we head to the concession stand.

She bumps me with her hip, trying to be playful. "I can't help but worry. You're not yourself."

I don't do a bump back. But I nod. Again, those tears are lurking like creepy stalkers. "I, uh, know." I bumble through my words. "Izzy, I just need . . . like really need . . . to get through this year and then I'll be good."

She slings her arm around me. "And you will."

"Of course, I wish Jada would break her leg or something and get all fat too, then I'd be so happy. Wouldn't it be great if she got badly injured and couldn't swim anymore?"

I can feel Izzy straighten up beside me. "Nova, that's a terrible thing to say."

"Oh, for god's sakes, I didn't say I want her to die. Just get fat and ugly like me."

* * *

Monday morning, I have a plan. I spent all weekend lying on my bed, thinking about it. I know Leo's schedule, and he has a spare second period — exactly the same time as me. I'm not sure if Jada does, but I will soon find out. I get dressed in my usual grey sweats and, fortunately, don't have to see either my mother or father, as they're both at work. I walk to the subway station, inhaling and exhaling, trying to get through every step. I stop at my favourite bakery and pick up a cheese bun and coffee for my ride. The weather is starting to shift and, by the odd shoot of green here and there, spring is on the way. Spring. Summer. Fall. Can't I jump through the months and get to fall now? With Leo and Jada out of my life, I'll be a lot better off. Jada's name in my brain makes me want to snap something in two, break something, throw something. I've never hated anyone until now. Senior year isn't what I thought it would be. I haven't been to a party since the one where I got wasted. I take a big bite of my bun, and the pastry melts in my mouth, giving me comfort, for a brief moment, anyway.

My first block at school flies by, and I concentrate. I wonder how Leo is doing without me tutoring him. I hope he's failing.

Class ends and my stomach feels sick, so much so that I feel little jabs, kicking me, telling me that what I'm going to do is wrong.

But I can't stop myself. I want to do this, and I don't want to. But something guides me. My feet just move. In the library, I duck behind the stacks and pretend I'm looking for a book. I hear them come in before I see them. They sit down and immediately open books. Heads bowed, they work, only taking time to compare notes. Work? Seriously.

The period ends and nothing. I know I'll have to wait now until Friday when there is another time that they have a spare together. What if they have a swim meet? Then she gets to post photos instead of me posting. Maybe I should start following them around school. Maybe they go before lunch, or after they've eaten? Or maybe they don't go there at all. That thought gives me a little comfort. Maybe he saved that spot just for us.

* * *

The rest of my week consists of me avoiding Izzy, following Jada and Leo as much as I can and spending time in my bedroom, either doing homework or scrolling through social media. I come across an article about a girl who took a photo of another girl in a change room and fat-shamed her. She got charged by the police. That won't happen to me. I'm a nobody with a nobody account. No one will care. Plus, I have a plan.

It all comes down to Friday. I do the same thing in second period and hide behind the bookshelves, waiting for my moment. Then it happens. They come in, sit down, do a bit of work, then I see him lean into her. I hear her giggle. I see them get up.

As soon as they leave, I follow. Since I know where they're going, and I also figured out there is a different route to the same back hallway, I take it. Once close to the private corner, I hear her whispering. And I hear his voice too, probably saying something about her hair and how good it smells. That rips me inside. Makes me steam inside too. I tiptoe toward where they are, staying hidden. All I need to do is peer around the corner and snap. I open the camera app and zoom in so I get a closeup. Then I step out and snap. Three shots.

They don't even hear me, they're too engrossed in what they're doing. I tiptoe down the long hall until I'm out of their earshot, then I pick up my pace, rounding a corner to find myself immersed in students walking the halls, heading to lunch. I try and make myself invisible in the crowds by glancing at my phone as I'm walking. The photos are good. He's got her up against the wall, her skirt hiked, his pants down. Oh yeah.

I stick my phone in my pocket and lift my head. That's when I see Izzy coming toward me. My throat dries. My heart pounds. Thank god I put my phone away before she catches me.

"Hey, wanna eat with us?" She's with Felix.

For the first time in ages, I say, "Sure."

* * *

When I get home from school that afternoon, I FaceTime Brad.

"Hey," I say. He looks tanned and relaxed.

"Hey, how are you? What's shaking?" He's walking down a street, and I swear I can hear the slapping sound of his flip-flops.

"Not much." I pause, then I say, "I have a favour to ask you."

"Shoot."

"I have a photo that I want to somehow put on the internet, but I want to make it look like it comes from another address. Yours is international."

"Okay. What kind of photo?"

"Just a photo."

He laughs. "That's a bit vague. What are you trying to do?"

"I told you, put up a photo, but I don't want anyone to know I posted it."

"Why? Is it a photo of people? Are you trying to be like those mean girls on bad television?" He laughs.

I sink into the mattress on my bed and exhale. That's exactly what I'm trying to be. How sick. How sad. What have I become? But then I think, no, they deserve it for all the pain they've caused me. "It's more like a vendetta and . . . they're deserving." I rush my words out.

"Nova, seriously." Brad shakes his head at me. "You're better than this. Don't put up some photo to get back at this chick who stole your boyfriend."

"I wish I'd never told you what happened."

"Well, you did. And I'm on to you. Don't do this."

"Says the guy who stole his parents' hard-earned money to fly off to a beach."

"That was a low blow," he says.

Since I can see his face, I can see the hurt in his eyes. I want to turn away, but I can't because we're doing FaceTime.

"Just for the record," says Brad. "I've been in regular touch with Mom and Dad, and I've already sent them over half of what I owe them."

I sit up in my bed. "They never told me that."

"I told them not to tell you about the money. I wanted to have it all paid off before I told you. Good on them for keeping the secret."

"Mom should have told me."

"Nova, they're worried about you. They kept asking me how you sound when we talk. I said sad, but you just went through a breakup. But now, I think I should be worried too. This is not like my kind sister to be so vindictive."

"Senior year sucks."

"Hang in there," he says softly.

"It's . . . not what . . . I thought it would be." I pause for a brief second. "When are you coming home?"

"When I've paid the money back, and I have money for my own place. I don't think there's room for me anymore."

"There's an extra bedroom. I can move into the small room and you can have mine. So . . . summer? Fall? When?"

"Nova, I can't answer that. I'm working hard, making as much money as I can. I'm applying for jobs back home and if I get one, I'll come back. And until then, hang in there, kiddo. Seriously, I want to see my sister."

"I need you here now! Don't you get it. I. Need. You. And I need you to help me with this photo."

"No. I won't do that. Look, I gotta go. But, please, don't do anything you'll regret. Your idea is a bad one."

"It's not that bad. She deserves it. Thanks for nothing!"

I hang up on him and lean back against my pillow, staring up at my ceiling. My body vibrates, I'm so mad. He won't help me. Mom and Dad didn't tell me Brad was paying them off. I want to get up, go question my mom or dad, but I can't get off my bed.

Instead, I stare at the photo again.

CHAPTER 25
SWEATPANTS CHICK

The photo stays on my phone until I print it off. I can't get the nerve up to post it online. Plus, I don't want Brad to find out, so I have a new plan. I decided to print it off and keep it hidden in my binder. It goes to school with me every day.

On April Fool's Day, I am rushing down the hall, staring at the floor when I feel the bump.

"Sorry," I mumble.

I look to see who I've bumped into, and it's Jada and Leo. My heart starts whacking against my chest. I try to do the dodge that I've perfected since I've been labelled *Sweatpants Chick*, but I'm not quick enough.

"Nova," says Leo. "Hi."

As soon as I hear his buttery voice, I look up. He stares at me and I see something there, like he's happy to talk to me, maybe, but then I shake my head. No. It's pity. I'm a fat pig and it's pity I see in his eyes. He feels sorry for me. It makes me shrivel inside. He used to look at me with love, affection, lust, like he thought I was beautiful. My hair always smelled like mangoes.

"April Fool's," I say.

Jada giggles. I stare at her. "Are you laughing at me?" I ask her. She immediately drops the smile. She shakes her head. "No

. . . I just thought you were making a joke, so I wanted to laugh."

I hold up my hands. "Yeah, right. So now I'm a joke."

She frowns at me and shakes her head. "I don't think you're a joke."

"No. But you feel sorry for me, right? Everyone feels sorry for me. I'm *Sweatpants Chick*."

"I don't call you that," says Leo. "I'm having a party this weekend. Why don't you come?"

I look away. "Like that's going to happen," I mumble. I had heard about the party. Izzy talked to me about it. She's going, but I don't want to. Not a chance.

He reaches out to touch my shoulder and I jerk away from him, sending my phone flying. It skids across the dirty school tiles. I'm trembling when I walk across the hall to pick it up. When it turns on, I breathe a sigh of relief.

"Is it okay?" Leo asks.

I don't answer and walk by them, head down, hair hanging in front of my red face. I walk straight to the restroom and hide in a stall. I'm sitting on the toilet, trying to breathe, when I think about the printed photo. My hands still trembling, I pull it out of my bag. Then I pull out a roll of tape. I get a pen and go to write April Fool's when I stop. No, they might recognize my handwriting.

I roll the tape, stick it on the back and put the photo on the back of the stall door.

Then I leave and head to class.

* * *

The next morning — which thankfully is a Friday — the picture in the restroom has been found and circulated. Everyone is talking about it, laughing about it and saying some nasty things. Guys are doing thrusting motions every time they pass Jada and clapping Leo on the back for being innovative.

I walk the halls all day and listen to what other students are saying about the photo. I feel as if I'm in my own secret world. There is talk, of course, that I was the one to do it. But when anyone asks me, I laugh and deny it. A bunch of students go down to the spot where Jada and Leo were caught in the act and take photos, putting them on social media with other memes.

Since I have no tutoring set up after my last class, I get my backpack and hurry to get out of the school. I'm almost out the front door when Izzy catches up to me. My only thought is to get home, and hide in my small room, behind my four walls.

"Hey," she says.

"Oh, hi."

She links her arm through mine and whispers, "Tell me that wasn't you." I purposely avoided Izzy all day, knowing she was going to ask me that.

I shake my head. "Nope. Wasn't me." I get a jab inside. A big jab. I've never lied to Izzy before.

She exhales. "Thank god. I didn't think it could be you. That's not who you are."

I can't look at her because right now, I have no idea who I am.

Izzy keeps talking. "I wonder who did it?"

I shrug. "Could have been anyone. Maybe someone just happened to see them there and thought it was funny. It is a pretty hidden spot." I give off a giant exhale. "Leo and I went there once."

"Ohmygod, you did?"

"Just once," I say.

She gives me a playful hip check. "I didn't know you had it in ya, woman."

"Yeah, me either," I say. Something shrivels inside of me. Why am I lying to my best friend?

CHAPTER 26
DRESS SHOPPING

Green grass sprouts. Little bursts of daffodils peak through the brown earth. The sun shines. April turns to May.

It's Friday, again (they seem to come and go like fleeting moments), and I've just finished Calculus when my teacher, Mrs. Bidell, asks me to stay after. Uh oh. Every time a teacher wants to talk to me, I wonder if it's because of the photo. I never got caught, they never caught anyone and it's kind of been forgotten. Or has it? Jada sent me a text message, telling me she knew that I had done it. And how could I be so cruel? Then she said Leo was extremely disappointed, and that karma was a bitch. Whatever that's supposed to mean.

"Nova," says Mrs. Bidell. "Thanks for staying."

"No problem." I try to act cool, but inside I'm a mess of sizzling wires.

"I just wanted to let you know that I'm getting fantastic reviews of your tutoring from parents. I wanted to say thank you for continuing to step up."

A huge wave of relief floods me. This isn't about the photo. "It's been good," I say. And it has been. The only good thing in my life, along with my grades. "I've enjoyed all the students."

"The comments are that their marks are so much better.

You're really helping them." She gives me a huge, bright smile. "You're on track to be valedictorian this year."

I nod, and desperately try to smile back at her. I wish I could jump up and down, because this is something I've wanted since I started high school. But I can't. I don't deserve the honour; not after what I did.

"Thanks," I say. "There's still another five weeks of classes, though, and final exams. I can't get too excited until final marks are out."

"Nova, you're always so humble."

If only you knew.

* * *

At the end of the day, I head outside by myself. It's a beautiful sunny day. The news of me possibly being valedictorian has given me a bit of a boost and I can almost feel heat from the sun. Something good in my pathetic life. As I'm walking, I feel cramps coming on. I stop moving and put my hand on my stomach. My period must be coming, finally. The stress of the breakup has made nothing be normal.

As I'm standing still, trying to deep-breathe to get rid of the pain, Izzy comes running up, looking fresh and happy. I can't remember the last time I felt fresh and happy. She often tries to catch up with me on Fridays, refusing to let me start my weekend alone. And I always tell her my weekend is packed. When it isn't. I'm home alone a lot. Ever since Valentine's Day, my mom and dad have been going out more to dinners and even movies. Sometimes they just go for a walk, holding hands. And they've taken a few weekends away as well. This weekend they're in Ottawa, visiting my grandparents. They talk about Brad all the time now, and how well he's doing. They've even said that they're proud of him.

"Nova!" Izzy smiles at me.

"Hey," I say.

"What a beautiful day." She holds her face up to the sun and inhales as if she's absorbing all the sunshine into her body. Then she exhales, glances at me and laughs. "Aren't you boiling?"

"Nope." Sweatsuits are still my wardrobe. I have to live up to my name.

"I've got a great idea," she says. "Since you've had the good news that you might be valedictorian, which I totally think is going to happen, I've been thinking."

Izzy is the only one I've told so far that I could possibly be the valedictorian. Again, I feel that kick of energy. Just a little bit.

"About what?" Izzy has been asking me, and asking me, to join her and Felix for grad. And I don't want to. I won't go.

"Let's go grad-dress shopping." She links her arm in mine. This is her third time asking me this.

"Let's not and say we did," I reply.

She stops and grabs me by the shoulders. She looks me in the eyes. I try to look away, but her eyes are like magnets. "I'm not taking no for an answer."

I'm hit with another cramp. "I'm not feeling so good," I say. "Period cramps."

"Told ya, it would take months to get you back on track again."

"No shopping."

"Come on, Nova. Let's go have fun. I will pick out a nice dress for you. At least something you can wear under your cap and gown."

"I'm not going out after, so who cares what I wear under my cap and gown."

"I do. Nova, you might be the valedictorian! You need a dress. I know you don't have anything in your closet to wear."

"Why, because I'm so fat?"

"You're not fat. You had a breakup and did a little too much stress eating. You'll lose it once summer hits and school's over."

"Hope so." I don't tell Izzy that I've actually been trying to diet the last couple of weeks, but it's not working.

"Pleeeease? Let's get you looking amazing for your amazing speech. Because I know it will be."

I think about that. Mom has said she wants us to go out after the cap-and-gown ceremony. I think she's even made a dinner reservation. She says she has a surprise for me. Maybe Brad is coming home! But the biggest thing about being valedictorian is that I can't wait to see Leo's face when he hears I got picked. Maybe I'll put a snide comment about him in my speech.

"Okay." I sigh. "But, for the record, I'm not going to the grad dance. I will go to the ceremony. That is the dress we buy for. Nothing long and fancy. I want a simple, short dress."

Izzy grins from ear to ear. "You won't regret this. Let's go right now! We'll do coffees first and have a girls' afternoon." She links her arm in mine and leans her head on my shoulder. "I've missed you." Then she laughs. "And I want you out of those damn sweatsuits. Retire them already. It's spring. Time for new birth!"

At the mall, with coffees in our hands, she drags me to Aritzia. I stop at the door, and refuse to go in. "I can't afford this store," I say.

"For god's sake, we haven't been out for months because all you do is tutor. Spend some of that hard-earned money, would ya? Maybe we can find a sale."

I groan. "Five things. That's all I will try on. And I will only try on if you try on too."

"I'm all for that," Izzy says. "My mom gave me some money to buy a new dress for the ceremony. I already have my grad dress."

I'm about to ask what it looks like when I see Jada walking down the mall with a few of the swim team girls. I don't want to see any of them.

"Let's do this," I say. "Before I lose my nerve." I push Izzy toward the front door of the store.

As we're walking in, I ask Izzy, "What's your prom dress like?" I want her looking on her phone, so she won't see Jada.

Izzy whips out her phone and gets immersed in finding a photo. *Please, don't come in this store.* I see Jada and her posse walk by. I exhale. But then I can't help but wonder what kind of dress she's wearing to grad.

Izzy finds the photo and shows it to me. Her prom dress is long, and a beautiful sapphire blue, slim fitting. No ruffles. No fluff. Strapless. It's totally Izzy. "It's gorgeous," I say.

Unfortunately, the feelings about not going to grad with Leo hit me hard. At the beginning of the year, Izzy and I looked at grad dresses together. Mine was going to be red. Yes, red. I wonder if Jada will wear red.

Izzy pulls me over to a rack of dresses. "This green would be beautiful on you." She takes if off the rack and hands it to me. "I'm going to be your stylist."

We each get a handful of dresses and take them to the back. The salesperson operating the change rooms puts us in rooms that are side by side. I shut the curtain, and I take the green one off the hanger. The size that Izzy gave me is at least a size up from what I normally wear. She did that without telling me.

I slip it over my head. It's a dress that has no waist but is the latest trend. Almost bohemian-like. It was belted on the mannequin. I don't want it belted. It has straps to hold it up, which I like. I step out and Izzy is in front of the communal mirror. She is wearing a tight, hot pink dress with spaghetti straps that looks amazing on her. She seriously is glowing.

She turns and looks at me.

Her gaze goes from my face to my stomach. Which is protruding out a little through the silk fabric.

I put my hands on my stomach. "I'm so bloated," I whisper. Not wanting the saleswoman to hear my personal stuff. "Told you, my period is on its way."

"The colour looks great," says Izzy. Her words come out with a forced enthusiasm. She heads into her cubicle change room and pulls the curtain across.

I'm moving toward my room, when suddenly, I hear the snap of a phone. I turn quickly and see Jada. She takes another photo of me staring at her before she holds up her phone. "Karma!" Her and her friends laugh.

I whip the curtain open and rush into my change room. My hands shaking, I shut the curtain tight. There's a small stool in the room, so I sit down. Another cramp hits me. I hold my stomach and try to breathe. Why does everything in my life hurt so much? When the pain subsides a little, I pick up my phone and go to my social media.

And there I am. In the green dress. The caption says:

I thought whales were grey!

OMG. I stare at the photo. Is that me? Really me? I'm huge. When did I get that big? How? I blink to stop the tears. How could she have done this to me?

Karma. I squeeze my eyes shut.

PART FOUR

MAY 9

I stand in front of two police officers, one female, one male, and there's also the fireman. The male police officer emerged from the police car as soon as he saw me walking toward them. I saw him get out of the car, almost as if he was afraid that I might do something crazy. But haven't I already? I have. I've done something awful. Just like I told Brad. I called Izzy. Where is she? No one is here with me.

I'm alone. Again.

I've done something so bad.

I'm like a crazy person. Only, I'm Nova. This isn't me. Or is it? What kind of person does what I've done?

I stand still and don't say anything more. Just stand there. I don't cry. I guess I'm done with that. I don't know. I'm numb inside. Numb outside too. It's like a light has been switched off inside of me, and I'm dark. I can't cry. I can't feel. I know I've done something horrible, though. I do know that. Why can't I cry?

I stare at the people standing in front of me. The police officers look so official in their uniforms with their bulletproof vests and guns in holsters. And the fireman too. Only he doesn't have a gun. I've never been in trouble before. I've never even been sent to the office at school. Ever.

I've always been a good girl.

A really good girl.

And now here I am, standing with the authorities. I'm tall, but they seem to tower over me. I feel small, like a child standing in front of their parents, not wanting to be in trouble. Only I'm not a child. And I am in trouble. Deep trouble.

"I don't want her to die," I whisper.

The female officer stares at me. "Why don't you tell me what you're talking about?"

"I never meant to hurt her."

"Hurt who?"

"Her."

CHAPTER 27
BLOOD

"I can't believe Jada did that to you," wheezes Izzy.

We're leaving the mall. I'm running. Izzy is trying to keep up to me. "I looked awful," I say. I'm still in shock.

Suddenly, I'm hit with another cramp and it takes my breath away. I put my hand on my stomach. I stop moving and double over with the pain. I keep trying to breathe, but I feel as if I'm hyperventilating. Air won't go to my lungs. I gasp and see stars. The pain is searing.

"Ohmygod. Are you okay?" Izzy asks. She pats my back. "Are you having an anxiety attack?"

I shake my head. The pain subsides. I breathe again, and I stand up. Sweat is dripping down my face. "I have the worst cramps. I'm going home."

"I'll come with you," says Izzy. "I know your parents are gone."

"No!" I almost yell right in the middle of the mall. Then I remember where I am. And I remember the photo. I want to be alone. That's all. "Izzy, please. Just leave me alone. I need to be alone. I need to be by myself."

"You don't need to be alone." She links her arm through mine, like we always used to do. "Nova, I'm your friend. Your best friend."

I jerk away from her. "Leave me alone, okay? It's not your fat body that's all over the internet."

"I'm just trying to help," says Izzy. She sounds so hurt. I look at her and see the concern on her face and I feel bad. I do. But I still don't want her coming home with me. I just want to curl up in a ball and fall asleep.

"I'm so sorry, Izzy. I am. But you can't help. I just want to go home. I'm going to be fine. I can handle this. Please understand."

"Nova. I think you need someone with you."

"Stop! You're always pushing me. I didn't even want to come dress shopping. This is your fault."

I take off running down the hall. Izzy follows and grabs my arm. I shake it off. "Leave. Me. ALONE!"

I keep running, down the stairs, out of the mall. When I don't hear her behind me, I slow a little. By the time I make it to the subway station, I'm almost delirious. Sweat seems to ooze from every pore in my body. The subway is packed but I get a single seat. I'm dizzy. The cramps have subsided a little. I look at my phone. Everyone is laughing at me. The whale. I'm a whale. I rock back and forth and try to breathe. We're almost at my stop and I'm hit with another awful cramp. I try to act normal, but I do put my head between my legs. It goes away, and I exhale.

I gotta get home. Get to my room.

As I'm walking to my apartment I stop twice, clutching my stomach, bending over with the pain. The cramps are getting worse. Did I eat something to make me feel this way? Or am I just reacting to being a fat whale on social media?

As soon as I walk in the apartment, I lock the door and head to my bedroom. If Izzy shows up, I won't answer. I'm so hot that I take off my grey sweatsuit and put on my biggest T-shirt before I flop down on my bed. Thankfully, my parents are gone. At this point I don't want anyone hovering over me, asking me if I want soup. I curl into a ball and rock back and forth. The pain is horrible. But it comes and goes. I hear my phone pinging. It's Izzy.

I text her to get her off my back.

I'm ok call you in am. Sorry for earlier.

As I lay on my bed, I go in and out of sleep. If only I could puke.

Finally, I wake up around two in the morning. An intense pain hits me hard, making me gasp. I get up to go to the bathroom. When I stand, I wobble on my feet. Another stab takes my breath away. I try to inhale and exhale. I sound like a horse. I grab my stomach. The hardness of it surprises me. Maybe I've got some weird parasite.

I edge my way down the hall, holding on to the walls. When I get to the bathroom, the pain has subsided a little bit. I sit on the toilet and just sit there. My skin is clammy. Sweat beads off my forehead, and drips down my back. This is the worst flu I've ever had. The worst pain ever.

As I'm sitting on the toilet, I have this odd feeling that I need to go to the bathroom. I wish at this point I would get diarrhea to get rid of everything in my stomach.

Suddenly, I let out a grunt. I can't control myself. A gush of water rushes out of my body.

I stand up. The pee soaks my legs.

But when I look down at them, I don't see pee. I see water. A puddle. Something is wrong. I hold on to the wall and just stand there. Another pain hits me. So hard I see stars in front of me. Dizzy, I fall to the floor and sit there, back against the wall. Trying to breathe.

Another pain hits and I scream out loud. Like shriek. Then I feel something between my legs. I pull them up to my chest. *Breathe, Nova, breathe.*

What is happening? I put my hand down there and feel something hard. I cry. Tears and more tears. Another pain hits me. I grunt again, like I'm an animal.

Something comes out.

Afraid to look, I put my head back. Another pain hits me. The feeling between my legs is like nothing I've felt before. I glance down.

I see a head.

CHAPTER 28
I KNOW WHAT IT IS

Another stab of pain. Another grunt.

A little red thing slides out of my body. I stare at it. Just sit there and stare. It is small. Wrinkly. Red. I know what it is.

I scream.

It just lies there. Tears rack my body. I sit on the floor and sob. Then I'm crushed with another horrible jolt of pain, like someone gouged me with a knife, and something else slides out of me. This red mound of blood. The floor is blood. All blood.

I look again at *it*. Is it dead?

I can't touch it. I just can't.

But then it cries. A piercing sound. How can something so small and ugly give off such a sound. Sobs rack my body. It stops crying. I can't stop though.

I see the cord attaching us together. I remember a movie or television show — I can't remember — where a woman had a baby and how they rushed her in. How they had to cut a cord. How am I to do this? Me. Here in my bathroom. But I must do something. Otherwise, it is connected to me. I know that much.

I want it gone. I want this to be over. I don't want it to be a part of me.

I glance at the cabinet above the sink and see scissors. I will cut. And then I will tie. I can do this. I'm going to be a surgeon. I have to lift it up to get the scissors. I manage to get them out of the medicine cabinet. It has stopped crying. Maybe it's dead.

It almost makes me sick to cut the cord holding us together. My hands shake as I knot it. I'm sure I'm doing the worst job ever. I don't want to touch it. But my fingers graze the skin of it as I tie the cord. It whimpers. Oh god, it's still alive. I snatch a towel off the rack. It needs to be covered, warmed up. Once wrapped in the towel, I pick it up. It's so small. And light. It has legs that look like chicken wing bones.

I sob. And sob. What am I going to do with it?

Now that the stabbing pains are gone, I manage to stand up. My stomach still throbs but the . . . other pains are gone. I can't bring myself to think I was in labour. Labour? Blood is everywhere. I will leave it and clean up later. I take it to my room and place it on my bed.

On my bed it looks like a toy. Its scrawny legs move a little. It does this weird movement with its face. Like a scrunch. Arms twitch. How am I going to do what I need to do? I have no choice. I put my grey sweatsuit back on.

My body is numb. My head fuzzy. I move as if I'm a robot. As if someone has pressed a button on my back. It's spring outside. I won't need a coat. But it needs a better blanket than a cold towel. I get one of my old sweatshirts from my closet and wrap it in that. Easier to get down my elevator with it wrapped in old clothes like I'm going to the recycling bins. It must stay quiet.

Since it's the middle of the night, there's no one in my hallway. Or in the elevator. I get to the ground level and hurry outside. It's a spring night, and the air is warm.

I rush down the sidewalk. I know where to go. Wrapped in my old hoodie, it is quiet. Maybe it died. From the distance, I see the lights on at the fire station. Easiest drop-off place. There's always someone there.

I glance around as I approach the fire station. What if someone sees me leaving it? No one can. No one. Where do I leave it? I feel movement under the hoodie. My stomach feels sick. I have to do this. Don't I? I'm going to university next year. Graduating soon. I want to be a doctor. Maybe even a surgeon.

More movement. Under the light of a streetlamp, I open the hoodie a little.

Its eyes flutter. It blinks. I hold my breath. I swear, in between the blinks it stares at me as if it knows what I'm going to do.

Then it closes its eyes and screams.

"Shhhhhhh." I hold it to me and try to stop it from crying. "Please, stop." I whisper. "Stop. You can't cry now."

I glance around. No one on the streets. I'm not taking any chances. I duck behind a tree and try to get it to stop crying by moving my arms back and forth. I used to babysit. I can do this. I see a hedge and a spot where maybe I can hide. After I'm tucked in the bushes, I wonder what would happen if I just left it here, lying on the ground.

It would die. I need to leave it somewhere else, so someone can find it.

As I sit on the ground, I put it against my chest. I want it to stop crying first. I can't leave it alone if it's crying. Its little body presses against mine. It stops crying and makes this weird suckling noise. I open the hoodie up and stare at it again. It's so small. So tiny. I know it's not full grown yet. Its eyes open again. And it stares up at me. Blinking. Then its eyes roll back in its head. It has no eyebrows or eyelashes. Does it know what I'm going to do?

Tears fall. I can't do what I want to do. I just can't. But I have to.

The church is always dark at night. I can't leave it there. But the fire station is open, all the lights are on. Fire stations are good places. Right?

What if it doesn't live, though?

I open the blanket again and look down at the "it" in my arms.

Then it hits me. This is not an *it*; she's a baby girl. Her tiny chest moves up and down as if she's struggling to get air. Just like me, always struggling to breathe.

"You can do this, okay?" I whisper to her. "Just keep breathing. Keep breathing. Keep breathing. That's all you have to do is breathe." I think of how Coach Maloney made me go over and over my breathing when I was swimming. "Just keep breathing, baby girl, keep breathing."

She quiets down, closes her eyes and her little chest goes up and down. She looks so small, so vulnerable, but yet . . . she's strong. I know that. I don't know why I do, but I do. Maybe stronger than me.

I cover her up so she won't be cold. I get off the cold, damp ground and stand. No one is coming down the street. Now's my chance.

With her in my arms, I run to the front of the fire station. I knock on the door. Hard. So hard my knuckles ache.

Then I leave her.

And run back to the bushes and peer through them. If no one answers I will go back and get her. I will. I'm about to make my move when the door opens. A fireman stares down, bends over, picks her up, stares at her, shakes his head, then shuts the door. I run home.

PART FIVE

MAY 9

The policewoman stares at me, up and down. I have changed into black sweatpants so I'm not dripping blood, although I'm sure it's there between my legs still, not that she could see in the dark.

"Are you her mother?" she asks me.

I can only nod.

"You left her there?"

"I didn't . . . know what to do. I didn't . . . know I was pregnant. I'm so sorry I left her. I'm so sorry." Just thinking of her, so little and scrawny, makes the tears return, falling down my cheeks like water over a cliff. "Is . . . she alive?"

"She's breathing," says the policewoman. She walks toward me. "I think we need to have a chat."

I nod. She ushers me to the back of the police car. I get in. She shuts the door. I sit there, alone in the police car. There are bars in front of me, like I'm some sort of criminal. But in a way, I guess I am. I abandoned my baby. If she dies, I'm a murderer.

Minutes later, or I think it's minutes, maybe it's not, I don't know, the policewoman opens my door and squats down in front of me.

"How about you tell me what happened?"

CHAPTER 29
MAY

Izzy arrives in her parents' car. I see her from the back seat of the police car. I've just told my story. How I had a baby without even knowing I was pregnant. How I left her because I didn't know what to do. How I came back because I realized leaving her was wrong.

"Nova," Izzy calls out, running toward me and the policewoman.

The policewoman gets up and stands in front of me, as if trying to block me from leaving the vehicle. Does she think I'm going to run away? Does she want to arrest me?

She turns and asks, "Do you know her?"

Izzy's face looks frantic. Funny, I don't feel frantic anymore. I almost feel calm. The male cop moves toward Izzy, stopping her from getting close to me.

"She's my best friend," I say. "I called her to come. She can take me to the hospital. I want to see the baby. Make sure she is okay."

"We do need to get you checked out as well," says the female cop.

"Can my friend take me?" The policewoman doesn't let Izzy get close to me. Hug me. I want to fall into her arms.

"It would be better if we did," says the policewoman. "But she can certainly follow us and be there with you, seeing as your parents are out of town."

I told the police officer that. That I was alone in our apartment. That my parents are in Ottawa, where my grandparents live. I also gave the police officers my parents' cellphone numbers.

"She was small," I say.

"Yes, she was." She stands up, closes the door on me again and walks over to Izzy. I see them talking from the back of the police car. Izzy nods and goes back to her car.

We arrive at the emergency entrance to the hospital, and I have to wait until they open the door for me because I'm locked in like a criminal. The policewoman escorts me in and talks to the receptionist, but I'm not in handcuffs. Izzy is beside me. I feel her hand take mine and give it a squeeze. People stare. I look down at the tiled floor.

I'm led to a room, and the policewoman says she will wait outside the door. Izzy is allowed in with me because I requested it and my parents aren't with me. The doctor makes me get up on the bed, and the white paper crinkles underneath me. I lie back and she checks me out. She's gentle and kind, and I appreciate that.

"All looks okay," she says. "You have a few tears, but nothing that won't heal in time." I hear her gloves snap off. She throws them in the trash can before she turns to me. "I'm guessing you were around thirty-two to thirty-three weeks pregnant."

I don't answer. I try to calculate back. Did I get pregnant on my birthday dinner? I sit up and cover myself. I close my eyes for a second, then I open them and whisper, "How is she?"

"Your baby girl is a fighter," says the doctor.

I stare down at the sheet that is covering my bottom half.

"How . . . much does she weigh?" I ask.

"She weighed in at just under four pounds."

Four pounds? I think of a four-pound weight at the gym. That weight was in my stomach. How could I not have known?

"I had my period," I say. "Well, not a full period, but blood for a day or so. I was on the pill."

"That could have been spotting," says the doctor. "Some women spot through their entire pregnancy."

"I thought I was fat."

"That's common too." She types a few things in a computer. Then she looks over at me. "You're also tall, so the baby could hide. And young so your skin is still elastic." She stands. "I'd like to get you to a room so we can monitor you."

"How could I not know?"

"It happens," says the nurse. "You're not the first, nor will you be the last."

"Will she survive?" My voice cracks.

"I can't answer that. But, as I said, you have a fighter. They will put her on a lung machine because she's premature. She'll be in the neonatal unit until they are sure her lungs are good. But . . . she was breathing on her own when she was brought in, which is remarkable." She smiles at me. "And she can cry."

"I, uh, had a night where I got really drunk." My shoulders start to shake.

"Only time will tell if that has any effect on her," says the doctor.

Izzy is suddenly by my side. "Don't go there, Nova. Not now."

I'm taken to a room, and Izzy comes with me. I wear the typical hospital gown. And I'm in a room with someone else. The nurse pulls my curtains around. As I lie on the bed, I stare up at the ceiling. Izzy holds my hand.

"You can go," I say. I roll my head to look at her.

She shakes her head. "Not a chance. Your parents are on their way too."

"What am I going to do?" Tears leak from my eyes. "What if I have to go to jail for abandoning her? What if she dies? I'll be a murderer."

"Let's hope that won't happen. You did drop her off someplace that you thought was safe." Izzy squeezes my hand.

"I left her at the fire station." My words hardly come out. "Maybe I shouldn't have done that. Why did I do that? Izzy, I was so shocked that . . . I just didn't think."

Izzy wipes away the tears streaming down my face. "You made the right decision to go back. I'm glad you called me, Nova."

"I'm sorry I pushed you away today." I close my eyes. "I guess I was a whale for a reason." Suddenly, I'm exhausted. So tired that I sink into the mattress.

I must fall asleep, because when I open my eyes, light is streaming through a window. And my parents are sitting by my bed. Now, my mother is holding my hand. And Izzy is gone.

"Nova," says Mom softly. She pushes a strand of my hair off my face.

I glance around. White sheets. White walls. Curtains. Plastic chairs. Where am I? Why am I here? I close my eyes again. Then it all comes back to me.

"I'm so sorry." I start to cry. Again. I can't help it.

"Shhh. It's okay." My mother continues stroking my hair. "Brad called us, and we came as quickly as we could. We were already on the road when the police called."

"I didn't know." My body racks with sobs. "I swear. I didn't. How could I not? And I left her. I left her alone."

"Let's not think about that now," says my mother.

My father gets up off his chair and holds my other hand.

"I want to go to university. Be a doctor. I don't want to go to jail."

"We're here for you," says my father. "We've already talked to the police. They're not going to charge you because you returned to find her."

"Is . . . is . . . she still alive?"

"She is," says my mother. "She's actually doing really well, considering."

"She's a fighter," says my father. He squeezes my hand. "Just like you." He lets go of my hand. "How about I get us breakfast?"

"That would be great," says my mother.

Dad leaves, and me and Mom are alone.

"What am I going to do, Mom?"

"You have two options at this point," says my mother. "You can keep her, or you can give her up for adoption. Dad and I will support you whatever you choose."

I nod. "It's a big decision."

"Probably the biggest you'll ever have to make."

"You're not disappointed in me?"

"No, honey. We're here to support you in whatever decision you choose. And if you decide to keep the baby, she will only enrich your life." She smiles at me. "Just like you've enriched mine."

CHAPTER 30
BIG DECISIONS

I don't want to keep her.

Or at least that's what I keep telling myself. But then I can't say the word — *adoption*. It won't come out of my mouth. How do I make such a big decision? I'm not cut out to be a mother. I want to be a doctor. But she came from my body. My mind is like a ping-pong ball, going back and forth.

"Are you ready to go?" My mother is at the foot of my hospital bed. I get to go home. I've only been in the hospital for an extra day. And now I've been given the green light that I'm physically fine. Baby doesn't get to go, though. Apparently, she's in some incubator, and has tubes. I've avoided seeing her. The policewoman came to visit me and told me that they weren't laying any charges. Had she died, I could have been charged with manslaughter. I could have gone to jail for what I did. She sure didn't make light of the situation. But Baby is still alive, breathing, holding her own in this big world we live in. She is saving me from a future in jail by continuing to breathe.

But I haven't even been to see her.

"I'm good," I say.

"Dad is waiting downstairs with the car."

I nod.

We leave the room, and head down the hall. I walk slowly. How can I just leave her again? I already did this once.

We stop to do the necessary paperwork at the desk. The nurse looks at me, and before I can stop myself, I say, "Can . . . I . . . see her before I go? Just to say goodbye." After I ask, a ball of something wedges itself in my throat. My body starts to tremble, and I feel sick to my stomach. Why did I even ask?

Because it's only fair to her. I'm her mother.

"I'll wait here," says my own mother.

"You're not coming with me?" I stare at her.

She shakes her head. "No, honey. I've said my goodbyes. Now it's your turn."

"Should I even do this?"

"Only you can make that decision."

Should I? Maybe not. But I think I should. After all, she came out of my body. As if I'm on some automatic pilot, I follow the nurse.

She leads me into a room full of incubators with scrawny babies in them. Most have tubes taped to them. Immediately, I spot her at the far end. I know her. I held her that horrible night. She blinked at me. I've had nightmares about that blink. Those eyes looking up at me as if they could read my mind.

"She's at the end," says the nurse.

"I know," I say. "Thanks." I walk slowly toward her.

When I get to her, the first thing I see is the card on her incubator that only says Foley, my last name. She doesn't even have a first name. I close my eyes. My heart beats. My pulse races. I take in a deep breath and open my eyes as I exhale. I stare down.

Oh god. Tubes are taped to her red, wrinkly, scrawny body. I can see her heart beating against her paper-thin skin. Up and down. Laboured, almost. I was told she needs oxygen. They have to keep her levels up. She has another tube where they feed her. Her legs still look like chicken bones. Tears sting my eyes. She's trying so hard.

This *baby* came from my body. And she's desperately trying to live.

A nurse walks over to me. "If you put your hands in the holes, you can touch her."

"Thanks," I say.

Do I want to do that? Touch her? I did touch her that night she was born.

I slide my hand into the incubator. My throat dries. My skin prickles. But . . . I reach out and touch her hand. It's hardly the size of my nail. She surprises me by curling her little hand around my finger. Tingles run from her hand through my body. Stronger tingles than those that would hit me when Leo touched me. These make my entire body vibrate.

Her eyes open. Then she rolls them back into her head as if she enjoys being touched. By me. I swear she smiles when she does that.

The same nurse comes by the incubator. "She likes you touching her. You can hold her if you want."

"Hold her?"

"I can take her out for you."

"I don't know if I can do that."

She shrugs.

"O-kay," I say quickly.

The nurse takes her out and puts her in my arms. "You've got one strong girl there."

I stare down at her.

I don't say goodbye.

CHAPTER 31
GOING HOME

I visit her every day. I learn how to change her. I watch them feed her. I hold her. Sometimes, it's a skin-to-skin hold because the nurses tell me that's good for her. To be able to go home, she needs to pass the car seat test. Keep up her oxygen while sitting in the car seat. I watch her fail. My heart breaks for her. But she doesn't give up. She keeps breathing. She keeps trying. I figure I should do the same.

After three times, she passes her car seat test. She can go home. I come back to the hospital, stay with her overnight, to prove that I can take care of her. This time we both pass the test.

It's morning and I sit with her in the rocking chair. I'm exhausted from being up with her all night. The chair goes back and forth. The creaking sound is mesmerizing. She's sleeping in my arms. I FaceTime Brad so he can see his niece. He's coming home in a month.

After hanging up, I look down at Addie. Whenever I feel overwhelmed (which is a lot), I think of how tough she is. She fought to breathe. She fought to suck a bottle. She's still fighting to breastfeed. All her fighting made me want to fight to keep her. So . . . I've been making plans. I used some of my tutoring money to buy a car seat and a bassinet. She will sleep beside me in my room. Mom is adamant that I be the one to take care of her. I'm scared. So scared.

I stare down at her. Today she is dressed in the pretty pink sweater and hat that Izzy knitted for her.

I haven't been back to school. All my teachers said I could finish my courses online. Next week, I'll write my exams with everyone else, though. There will be a lot of people staring at me, whispering. I'll have to handle it. I've also decided to go to the grad ceremony. Not the dance, though. Mom and Izzy even went shopping and bought me the green dress.

I'm still giving my valedictorian speech, even though I told the principal that I was the one who put the picture of Jada on the bathroom door. The teachers had a meeting to vote about whether I should be allowed to give the speech. Only one teacher felt I shouldn't.

I recite my speech to Addie.

We are all closing a chapter in our lives and moving on. As we go forth, life will be full of surprises. I'm proof of that. (I know that'll make the audience laugh, and it's okay. That's what I want.) Some big. For me, huge. (Pause. Maybe more laughter?) But some small too. Some of you might follow one path. And that's amazing. You'll have a goal and you'll reach it. But, here's the thing, some of us may not just follow one path. And that's okay too. Sometimes we might have to take a detour, and it might take us longer to get to our goal. But that goal will be waiting. Or . . . maybe there'll be another goal there. One that is a surprise. Coping with the surprises in life will be our biggest challenges.

I'm still talking and rocking her when I hear footsteps. I turn around, expecting Izzy or even Felix, but that's not who I see.

Leo.

He has his hands shoved in his pockets. He looks so sheepish. After four weeks, this is Leo's first visit to see me. To see her.

"Nova," he says.

"Leo." I look up at him.

Since Addie is asleep, I put her back in her hospital bassinet.

He stares at her. "Wow. This is so weird."

"Yup," I agree. "Surreal."

He eyes me. "You really didn't know?"

"I'm sure rumours have been flying around the school," I say. "But I didn't. That's the truth. Maybe I wasn't looking, though." I shrug. "I'm still in shock."

"Are you . . . keeping it?"

I nod. "*It* is a girl. Her name is Addie."

"Yeah . . . I think I heard that."

"I bet you've heard a lot," I say.

"I was away swimming." He looks away. "National Team tryouts."

I reach in the bassinet and put out my finger. Addie grabs on with her small hand. "I heard you made it," I say.

"Yeah," he says. "I did." He pauses for a second. "I don't know what you want me to do." He runs his hand through his hair.

I shrug. Then I stare at Addie. She has a firm grasp on my finger. "That's up to you."

"Since you didn't let me have a choice in the decision, I don't think it's fair that you expect anything from me."

I let go of Addie and turn to Leo. I stand up tall, facing him head-on. Since having Addie, I've thought a lot about Leo. Him not coming to see me just doesn't cut it in my books.

"I don't expect anything from you." I pause. "And just an FYI . . . if you wanted to be a part of this decision, you should have come weeks ago. You couldn't be bothered to see me, no, see *us*, so I don't owe you anything. I sent you a text. And I phoned you. And left a message."

"I had a meet. I've been gone for two weeks."

"That's not an excuse. I've made my decision to keep her without you."

He stares at Addie for a second but quickly looks away. "What about university? I thought you, uh, wanted to be a doctor."

"I'll still do that. Next year, I'm going to take a few in-person classes and do the rest online. My mother will care for her while I'm at school. I'm not giving up on my dreams."

"You know I have to go away, right? I've already accepted my scholarship."

"That's your choice, Leo. But any time you want to visit her, I'll be okay with that. You are her father. I realize things could change down the road. One day she might need you more than you know."

"Okay, yeah, maybe. Let's cross that bridge later, okay? I don't disagree, but I just can't absorb this right now. My parents said they'd help financially for a bit anyway. While I'm in school." He shuffles his feet. "Well, I should get going."

"Yes, you go," I say. "Before you go, though, I want to apologize for my actions. I'm sorry about the photo. That was so wrong of me to do that. And I'm sorry for how I behaved, the things I said to Jada. I want to blame it on hormones, but that's no excuse."

"I'm sorry too, Nova. Sorry we didn't work out. And sorry that I just can't help you with this. Right now, anyway. I'm not saying never though. Just give me time to process it all."

I watch him walk away from me. From us. I look back at Addie. I pick her up.

"We're okay," I say. "You're teaching me how to be a fighter."

She coos. Yawns. And closes her eyes.

And breathes.

So I breathe too.

ACKNOWLEDGEMENTS

Thank you to Carrie Gleason for chatting with me at the Ontario Library Conference about this idea, and for her fine editing and publishing skills. And to Kat Mototsune for the first edits on this novel, and thinking Nova and Leo were strong characters. The design team at Lorimer did a fantastic job of the layout and cover and I thank them for all their artistic help. The sales team chimed in on the cover and marketing will help promote the book. Thank you to my fabulous friends Karen Spafford-Fitz, Natasha Deen and Dannica Valant for their cover input as well.

A huge thanks goes to Andrea Opdebeeck for answering all my questions on the ending of the story. I don't want to give the story away so I can't tell exactly what Andrea helped me with, just know she was a huge help. Thanks to my RCMP friend, Janice March for her help in making the story correct.

I'm lucky to have a wonderful agent, Amy Tompkins, from Transatlantic, who champions my work and has great insight and thoughtfulness.

Thanks to all the booksellers, bloggers, reviewers, teachers, librarians, and parents who encourage reading. We writers need readers, so we love when you spread the word about our books. That's why we write.

And that leads me to you readers!

Thank you so much for reading. Please enjoy!!!